Heart
& Soul

D1458565

Heart & Soul

Liz Rosenberg

Harcourt Brace
& Company

San Diego
New York
London

Requests for permission to make copies of any part of the work should be mailed to: Permissions Department,
Harcourt Brace & Company, 6277 Sea Harbor Drive, Orlando, Florida 32887-6777.

The anecdote of the iron mask was drawn from Heather McHugh's poem "What He Thought" in *Hinge and Sign: Poems, 1968–1993*, published by the University Press of New England.

Library of Congress Cataloging-in-Publication Data
Rosenberg, Liz
    Heart & soul / Liz Rosenberg.
        p.   cm.
    Summary: Seventeen-year-old Willie Steinberg returns home to Richmond from a private school in Philadelphia depressed and overwhelmed, but as she helps an eccentric fellow student, she begins to have a better understanding of her parents and of her own musical talent.
    ISBN 0-15-200942-6
    ISBN 0-15-201270-2 (pbk.)
    [1. Parent and child—Fiction.   2. Jews—United States—Fiction.   3. Music—Fiction.   4. Richmond (Va.)—Fiction.]   I. Title.
PZ7.R71894Ch   1996
[Fic]—dc20   95-23569

The text was set in Bodoni Book.

Designed by Linda Lockowitz

First edition
A B C D E
A B C D E (pbk.)

Printed in Hong Kong

I worked on this novel, off and on, for about fifteen years—there are many good men I want to thank for help along the way: the late novelist John Gardner; Ved Mehta; my father, Ross; my husband, David, and our son, Eli. But all the same this book is dedicated to that first, fierce friend, my mother.

Heart
& Soul

Chapter One

ALL THAT SPRING our house felt like a doctor's waiting room—even the bittersweet smell was the same, and the outdated magazines piled on tables, the long shadows stretching down the parquet floors. My mother stayed home, hoping for word from my wandering father. In Richmond the mail never came before eleven and sometimes not till three in the afternoon, but she would wait for the mail truck to round the corner, lifting a spray of rainwater that rose and fell like piano music. My job was to wait with her.

It was an impossible task, and trying to do the impossible can make you crazy. I was tired of waiting. I was seventeen years old, a would-be musician, not much of a talker. My hands shook, my mouth shook when I tried to eat or speak, but I don't think anyone saw that. It was a very quiet time.

My parents had bought the house in Richmond, Virginia, three years earlier, when I'd gone to a private high school of music and art up in Philadelphia, and my mother seldom went out, so we were still strangers there. We didn't know anyone, and no one knew us. The name of our street was Gardenia; it was last on the mailman's route.

Whenever my mother and I crossed paths in the house, we reacted in mimed polite horror, like strangers bumping together in a museum. When we came together for supper, we all but shook hands. I had just dropped out of school in the middle of my senior year in Philadelphia and came back to Richmond jumpy and underweight, with what I called a bad cold, and a face in the mirror that looked like an advertisement on poor mental health. I wasn't volunteering any more detailed information than that, and my mother wasn't asking any questions.

The night nurse up at school didn't think it was a cold. She was the last person I saw before I went home. She held me against her stiff, sweet-smelling white uniform and told me to "let it all out." It made me think of what I'd been reading about in Italian history. There was once a musician, a revolutionary who had become so beloved among the people that the government decided to put him to death. But they were terrified of what he might say to the people at his execution, and so they decided not to let him speak. They made an iron mask so that he couldn't be heard. And he went to his death wearing the iron mask. It's a gruesome story, but I envied that musician for three reasons. One, he only wore that mask at his death. Two, he didn't put it on himself. And three, whatever he couldn't say—because of the iron mask— what he didn't say; that was music. I had the mask, but no music. Just the mask.

I moved my cello into a sun-filled front parlor that had been my father's study when he still lived with us, and carted out his papers and pharmaceutical catalogs, tore the atlas off his wall and the map indicating the depths of all the waters of the world, and dumped it all in a dusty corner of the attic. I didn't want to leave anything behind that felt or smelled like him. My grandfather's Baldwin resided in the parlor, so I turned the place into a music room: organized back issues of *Musical America,* set out the *Harvard Dictionary of Music,* had the piano tuned, and rigged up an architect's elbow lamp, placing it carefully so the bulb didn't shine right into my eyes or cover the paper with distracting shadows.

Sometimes my mother would catch me wandering the halls and ask if it was all right for me to be missing so much school, but she didn't push me, didn't even look me in the eye. She was half in a fog herself. She'd forget to turn over the charred lamb chops or shell steaks we had for supper, with half-frozen peas we'd chase around the plate onto our forks. Then later, after I'd cleared the dishes and even the cicadas had fallen silent, she'd sit at the kitchen table, her back erect, her blond hair gathered up into one fist, travel brochures fanned out in front of her like a hand of solitaire: brooding, hoping, laying schemes.

My father stayed away from all this. He was off on business: no permanent phone number, no forwarding address. He'd been appointed executive vice president of sales to a large pharmaceutical corporation based in Richmond, but for two years his business had taken him every place but home. He stood stoop-backed at six foot five—I got my own freakish height from him—and he had an unreliable heart valve my mother worried about. I didn't worry about it; I hoped he'd die.

He had risen slowly through the ranks of his business, putting one Italian leather shoe on the corporate ladder, then another, and the last we'd seen of him he was still climbing away, his jaw clenched. In the brick building of his first pharmacy in Hartford, he had measured, bottled, weighed, and advised while perspiration darkened the back of his long white coat, encircling the armholes and spreading over the shoulder blades—an angel of hard labor. As he advanced from one promotion to the next, his dedication rose to greater and greater heights, till at last, in the year of which I am writing, he seemed in danger of vanishing altogether on those shopworn wings.

He sent us postcards from the picturesque spots he was always passing through, or near. Once every three or four weeks he phoned.

Then my mother would shut the door to her bedroom and the tremor in her voice would find its way past the thrum of her air conditioner to the landing, where I paced back and forth by the front door, ready to run. If I didn't slip out in time, I had to talk to him on the extension downstairs.

"How's my girl?" my father would ask. The heart condition left him permanently short of breath, so he always sounded as if he'd been running. The accent was backwater Maryland, with a twang on the upbeats.

"I'm all right." I held the phone receiver a foot from my mouth, trying to sound as far away as possible, remind him about long distance.

"Semester's not over yet, is it?"

"No sir."

"You know, that isn't an inexpensive place we're sending you—" He'd pause politely, not wanting to directly mention money.

"I have bronchitis."

"I thought a cold."

"Bronchitis," I repeated with exaggerated patience. "But I'm fine."

"How's your mother?"

"She's fine, too."

There'd be a silence, during which we could both hear her quietly breathing on the line.

"Well, good. So everything's fine there, no problems, no—"

"We're both fine."

"Okay." My father would wait for me to say anything else, then give up with a weary cough. "Okay, Willie. You should be hearing back from colleges soon. Don't let your senior year slide. Try gargling with an antiseptic, all right? You know what to do. Get better soon."

Then he would hang up, and after a few seconds my mother would hang up, setting the phone down gently, and then finally I would, too. I had not actually applied to any colleges yet, and at this rate it didn't look like I was going to graduate from high school. But I didn't talk about that to anyone, either.

In Richmond I felt like an Amazon, a Yankee invader, though I dutifully wore the shirtwaists my mother bought at Thalheimer's and laid out on my bed. They hung above my knees like flowered bedsheets, ruffled at neckline and hem. I stood over six feet tall in my stocking feet. The dresses only pointed up how unlike I was the young women of

Richmond in their cool-looking cottons and polyesters. The men kept themselves dapper and neat even in the wilting April heat. They looked about as remote as the Elgin Marbles, and almost as friendly.

Yet still—there was a world of sociability humming all around us, on every side. You could hear it in the aisles of the Winn Dixie, where pregnant housewives leaned over their carts to chat, and at city bus stops; even in the sly, half-angry joking exchanges between old men at the corner cigarette store I wandered in and out of every day, invisible and dumb.

Sometimes I'd catch sight of myself looming up in a plate-glass window; my face shut down and sullen, my big hands jammed into my dress pockets—not a pretty sight. I reminded myself about the famous story of Beethoven plunging through a crowd of Austrian aristocrats while his walking companion, Goethe, stood off to one side, devoutly tipping his homburg hat. But I was the enraged musician *and* the respectful servant of social order—both, that is, and neither; I was no one and nothing at all.

Richmond had its own life, independent

of mine, with an older, European feeling. Its houses, churches, and banks rose up around me on all sides, as rich and unreachable as they seemed in the leather-bound books of my grandfather's music library. I crouched over his old Baldwin as if it were a Ouija board, trying to get running starts on bits of music that dissolved under me at a touch—the same three or four feverish notes with a high-pitched *blat* going up at the end. My high school music education had been devoted to this kind of thing; twelve tones and disso-nance, the new microtonics that were almost inaudible to anything but the computers on which they were composed. That was what earned the A's and music scholarships to good universities. I hated it all. I hated my century and myself for having been born in it. The one musician I believed in was Beethoven. I believed in him like a religion —I wanted to *be* Beethoven, so I hammered away on the piano till my neck stiffened and my fingers curled up with fatigue, trying to work myself into a first symphony in the key of C for my graduating senior project—noth-ing less grandiose would do—racing against my eighteenth birthday on the fourteenth of

July, a date I thought of as the end to all hope.

But I tore up everything I wrote—before I could even hear the notes in my head; crumpling the heavy paper into balls and firing them at a wastebasket halfway across the room. Sometimes I'd play scales, or kid stuff —"Chopsticks" or "Heart and Soul." A plaster of Paris bust of the handsome young Mozart—a junior high school graduation present from some sadistic aunt—smiled coolly out over my head.

As soon as it got dark outside, I went for walks, driven out of the study by the staff paper piled up around me, the freshly sharpened pencils laid out in the shining grooves of the piano stand. In the evenings, my father's presence loomed everywhere—his name on the mailbox, his car still parked at the curb. Through a doll-size window in the side porch I could see my mother sitting at the kitchen table in her nightgown and robe. In front of her were travel brochures from China, India, Africa, and Japan; each pamphlet with its own different bright-colored border. She had also begun poring through catalogs from every college in America with a good music program. They sat next to my breakfast cereal, untouched, and waited patiently for dinner or dessert.

She frowned, lost in thought, shuffling through brochures as if they were cards in a tarot pack, lifting up one leaflet and setting it down again, or moving it under the light where she could see it better. Among the travel brochures, East Africa's, with a border the blue of a northern summer sky, found its way to the top of the pile most often—an exoticism that worried me. She sighed, licking her finger, turning pages. Her reading glasses lay folded next to her hands on the marble tabletop.

Richmond was beautiful at night, though foreign; given over to its historic ghosts, the unofficial city fathers—those fourteen gloomy, incandescent statues of Civil War heroes lining Monument Avenue. They gazed over the tops of the lampposts: Confederate generals Stuart, Jackson, Lee, and the rest. The warriors astride rearing horses had died gallantly in battle; those on horses with one raised hoof had been wounded in action; but the soldiers on beasts that stood placid, four-footed in any weather—the saddest-eyed and most mysterious heroes of all: those men had died at home defeated in their own beds. I walked past them down the wide, tree-lined streets, letting my sneakers fill up with rain-water, then turned where the avenues fanned out, tapered down to finger width in the distance, stopped like me, forgot themselves, and were lost into narrower streets, into darkness.

One night I was almost home from such a walk, turning in at the corner of Gardenia, when a voice called out to me. It was a husky sound, not male or female. When I looked around, no one was there. I'd been wandering around the neighborhood, passing lit windows and parlors with their blue TVs on, all the while trying to invent a lofty musical theme (preferably something in C major), but there was nothing left in my head anymore, not even other people's music. The inner silence was terrifying. It was a final step down a long ladder I'd been descending all fall and winter. A feeling of loneliness had settled deep in my bones, and if I'd come up against a real attacker I think I'd have fallen half gratefully, without a sound, like the tree in the forest when no one is there to hear.

But no phantom hand reached out for me. A cool wind hissed by, rattling the leaves, shaking an insubstantial rain over my hair. I cleared my throat, turning up the collar of my jacket. "Oh, well," I said, and the rough sound of my own voice startled me.

"I'm right over here," someone said. There was an unspoken "you fool" after it.

An old woman leaned over her porch railing at Gardenia and Harve. She waved, and something glittered under the porch light. I hesitated and waved back.

That instant she began floating lightly across her porch, gliding horizontally, like a ghost, without stirring out of her seat or turning her head to either side. My head went chilly and light. I watched her drift toward me but couldn't move to get away. When she had reached the top of the porch steps and seemed about to float on directly down the walkway at me, I saw her wheelchair gleaming under the light. She parked it with a snap of the brake. "You all live over on Gardenia, don't you?" she said.

My nerves were shot. All the jitters of the past year or so drew in at one point on her dead-white forehead.

"Do you have a name?" she asked.

"Willie." For some reason, I laughed when I said it, like the village idiot.

"Willie?"

My real name is Grace Willa—the one I was born with, not one I admitted to. "Willa," I said. "Steinberg."

"A relation to the great Pittsburgh conductor? —Or to George Steinberg, by any chance, senior vice president of Richmond Savings?"

I shook my head, "Sorry," I said, pretending to think about it. Maybe I was related to both and had just forgotten it.

"The bank is on Water Street," she added. "George's son-in-law is the councilman who wanted to make our street lamps orange, like those lamps they use to keep french-fried potatoes warm. You're new to Richmond, I gather?"

I said that I was.

"My grandmother was a stranger when she came up from Montgomery. She was a new bride, twenty years old. She wrote poetry. A lonely woman. I suppose that's how old you are."

"I'm almost eighteen," I said.

She nodded. "Later in life she developed a nervous condition and they had to send her on to Williamsburg. —You're making some friends here, I hope?"

I assured her I had loads of friends and snuck a look at my watch, a cheap one that I could not read in the dark.

She tapped something against her railing, and her raspy voice grew peremptory. "In the midst of everything else, my flowers need thinning. I know it's late, but it won't take a moment." She lifted a pair of garden shears. "And you *are* a neighbor." She said this last bit defiantly; it was her trump card. She was staring at me so fiercely she looked cross-eyed.

I came up her porch ramp—a rotting, weathered board laid next to her front steps —and took the shears from her hand. Her fingers were badly swollen and gnarled. She withdrew the hand quickly when she saw me look at it and buried it in the folds of her skirt.

"Just trim the tallest few along the edge of the drive," she called after me. Her breath followed with a wheezing sound, a saw cutting through wood. "The hollyhocks have single . . . cerise . . . flowers. They won't need but a little thinning—a few are white."

Then I was standing in the middle of her driveway, shears in my hand, with no idea what I was doing there and no idea how to thin a flower. It sounded like a surgical procedure.

"Cut above the side branches." Her voice carried as if she were standing right next to me.

I bent over what might or might not be a flower and closed the blades. Something soft-blossomed toppled into my hand. Leaves and stems glimmered into visibility under my fingers. Every time I cut one stalk another sprang up in its place, behind or beside it. My hands were cold. I began to think I would go on all night, razing the flower bed to the dirt while the sun slowly rose and the old woman slumped dozing in her wheelchair— that I would be found the next morning still circling around the driveway, a high school dropout, a Yankee and a confirmed flower thief, plucking numbly at the bare ground. But my neighbor broke the silence with a sound as harsh as a crow. "Thank you, young lady! —Thank you. Stop. That's surely enough!"

I straightened, fully vertical again. My head buzzed. I walked back up the ramp and gave the old woman an armful of flowers and the wet shears. My hands were as numb as if I'd been holding them in a tub of ice.

The old woman didn't say anything at first. She shook the water from the shears. "Well, goodness," she said in a dazed voice. "Just look, you've cut the little Connecticut Yankee delphiniums, too!" She kept turning the mass of dripping flowers over in her lap with one hand. Then she seemed to rouse herself. "Will you accept a few of these"—she detached some stalks from the rest—"for your poor mother? I don't visit much." She gestured at the wheelchair.

I reached for the flowers, but at the words "your poor mother" froze in place, one arm stuck out in the air.

The old woman leaned forward, wheezing hard. "You're the musician, aren't you?" she said. "I've heard you at the piano long hours. I once played, too, Delius and Chopin. Now and again I open my window to hear you better."

I felt myself blush. "That piano's completely out of tune," I mumbled, still staring at the bouquet she held out toward me. "There's nothing wrong with my mother. That piano's lousy, it's no good, I wish—"

"Be glad," she said. "The way you play—with great care and fire—you just lack confidence! If you had been one of my students, you would have been one of the truly great ones . . ."

She reached out and tapped my hand. She had an intent, distracted look on her face. "You will give great happiness to many people someday, and there is nothing finer than that. Nothing. I envy you." She slurred her words. I strained to hear her. A tight, desolate space in my chest seemed to crack open. Her head dropped forward. I thought she had fallen asleep suddenly, like an oracle. On the cast-iron table at her side was a glass of clear liquid with ice.

She reached for my arm and held it, leaning forward. Her breath smelled petrifyingly of some medicine: no, not medicine—it was spirits, gin. The old woman was drunk.

"Let go," I said, tugging my arm free. "You don't know what you're talking about."

Her head jerked up. She looked bewildered. "I need to be inside—"

I pushed her front door open with my hand, pretending it had nothing to do with the rest of my body. A familiar, lonely, flowerlike scent drifted out into the air, as if, like me, it had been waiting for this one chance to escape. Under the frame of the door the old woman stopped and craned her neck to look back at me. Her face was waxy and debauched, puffy around the mouth and eyes. She may have read something in my look, for her own expression changed. She pushed the flowers into my hands. "Good night," she said. "I doubt we'll meet again." She wheeled herself in and shut the door from the inside, with a click of the latch.

Next to my front stoop I lifted the lid of a garbage can and dumped the flowers in. They made a fluttering noise, like dead moths falling inside. Then I went upstairs to my room, where I lay on top of the sheets, staring into the blackness and holding my body very still, as if I were lying at the edge of a pit. I played an old childhood game to lull myself to sleep, reciting forward from A to Z by the names of the composers: Audran, Beethoven,

Chopin, Delius . . . and then backward: Zu-
kofsky, Yemen . . .

After that I didn't go out as much at night.
Whatever armor I wore during the day seemed
thinner at night; the voice of reason broke. So
I took my walks during the day, while my
mother hung around downstairs in her robe
and nightgown waiting for the mail.

The old woman down the street was true
to her word—I didn't see her face till a long
time later—but sometimes as I passed her
house I'd hear a piece of classical music
pouring out of her open window—one time
Mahler, another time Rachmaninoff, Chopin's
études. The volume was cranked all the way
up; the speakers faced the street—it must
have startled the neighbors. But for me those
days, it was the closest thing I had to a
conversation.

And now I found a new reason to stay
home at night. After midnight you could get
late-night classical radio stations from as
far away as New Orleans or Rochester—
dim, underwater voices, sputtering static—
with young musicians playing new work live
on the air. The best ones I'd look up and note
down jealously in my favorite Schwann cata-

log, which I kept by my bed like a family Bible. Some of the young composers were writing melodically, and a few wrote so beautifully that as I was listening, hands clenched, I didn't know if I was more terrified that they would make a mistake or that they wouldn't. The catalog otherwise fell open automatically to the Beethoven listings.

All my earnings from playing that year in a Philadelphia civic orchestra I had spent on an expensive, bicentennial edition of Beethoven's complete works. It was eternally lost in the mail somewhere, after a long, irregular correspondence with the company's computer. But now I had the radio at night, and I learned to steer by it the way sailors do by stars. The programs went on for hours. I'd fall asleep to static, or to ghost music riding in from the next station over, till the local news came on in the morning and startled me awake.

I kept books of poetry on the bed stand, too, in order to have something solid there when I woke; mostly my mother's anthologies of flowery nineteenth-century verse, left over from her college days. Mornings were the worst time of day for me; as if something had torn loose during the night and threatened to take me under with it as soon as I opened my eyes. I'd lift a book up onto my chest and leaf through the pages, saying certain lines out loud, but quietly, so my mother wouldn't hear. "To strive, to *seek*, to find, and not to *yield!*" The books were so old they fell apart in my hands, the pages splitting down the middle like dry, overblown roses.

A few hours every day I'd sit in front of the piano, worrying about finishing my senior project, not writing a single note, serving time. The composition paper rested against an old piece of stiff cardboard I'd saved from one of my father's shirt packages a few years earlier and propped against the piano rack. Some days even the piece of cardboard was too much of him to have around. I was easily distracted, especially by noise, and the warm spring air droned with motorcycles and car engines and the ringing of bicycle bells. At each sound I'd jump up and stand at the French windows, pressing my forehead against the warm glass. From there I could see the backboard where my father and I used to shoot baskets. I found myself watching for the mail truck through the leaves of the trees, keeping my mother company on the sofa downstairs. I was waiting for something, anything at all to come along and rescue me.

"Grace!" my mother called. She was sitting in the shade of the front porch. I was carrying a carton of cigarettes and the Richmond newspaper. "There's a letter for you!"

I tried to wave her into silence, but it only made her shout more loudly, more jubilantly.

"Willie, a *letter!*"

She made it sound like the first we'd ever gotten. Even our neighbor, a surly retired army colonel, cut off his lawn mower engine and looked at me pityingly.

I broke into a trot, picking up the pace before my mother could shout any more about our personal lives into the street. The letter might be news about the lost Beethoven collection—or an announcement that I'd won the BMI Young Composer's Award I'd neglected to apply for. "Your talent is such that it has come to our attention—" I'd invented letters of admiration from Samuel Barber and Leonard Bernstein; a full explanation and apology from my father; acceptances from music programs I'd never applied to; a federal grant commissioning my first symphony—I still believed salvation was going to descend upon me one day in some such form. Then again, it could be bad news.

I nodded absentmindedly to the neighbor, forgetting that our two households never spoke. "How y'all doing?" he asked, leaning heavily on the lawn mower handle. His grim look may have come from the plastic handle pressing up against his stomach, but it seemed to suggest I'd lost my music scholarship at school, that I was washed up at age seventeen, and my father had been found dead and laid out in another city.

"Isn't this fun?" my mother called. Her hand fluttered the envelope back and forth in the shade.

It was hot by May, and muggy, even for Richmond. Sometimes the whole city smelled like a barbecue; other times, like a funeral parlor—sickly sweet in the middle of the afternoon. I didn't want to read the letter anymore. It was important for me to try to stay calm and relaxed. I climbed slowly onto the porch and took the cool-looking grayish blue envelope out of my mother's hand and just held it for a second.

The name *Randolph* stood in the left-hand corner: round slanted letters, green ink. Relief rushed through me. It was nothing. Katherine Randolph was just a girl I knew up at school in Philadelphia, the friend of an almost-friend. She lived in Richmond, too, in the good, older neighborhood several blocks from Gardenia. Her great-great-grandfather had founded the Confederacy, or some such thing. I pulled out a thin, engraved white card and scanned to where she'd written a few sentences. "Please convalesce swiftly. M. Gelb invited to the fete also. It was nice writing to you, bye!" She had scrawled her name so the last loop of the *e* in *Katherine* ran off the bottom edge of the card. Up the side she had added a postscript: "I hope you are happier now." I folded the card in half and stuck it in the pocket of my dress.

My mother sat on the creaky porch swing with her bare feet tucked under her. The chains were old and rusted, and the seat hung crooked. She kept saying my father would fix it when he got home. She was smiling brightly, which deepened the lines around her mouth and eyes. She looked like a youthful fifty-year-old, instead of a woman not yet even forty. There was a pitcher of lemonade and vodka on the table in front of her.

"What is it?" she asked. "You have on such a peculiar expression."

"It's nothing," I said. "An invitation."

Her smile grew dangerously bright.

I took the card out and looked at it again. "Some girl I know is having a party. Her name is Katherine Randolph. Black tie or costume." I glanced up. "I think she's a debutante," I added.

"I should say so." She set her feet down, stopping the swing. *"Randolph* . . . that's a familiar name. Doesn't she have some kind of disease?"

I stepped back, feigning horror. "A *social* disease?"

"No," she said. "Come on, Willie. Something . . . an illness—your friend Malachi Gelb told me, up at school. Something horrible."

"There's something horrible about Malachi," I said. "And he's not exactly my friend."

"He *would* be if you'd let him. —Well,

the party sounds nice." She sounded wistful.

I frowned. "It sounds stupid."

She looked as hurt as if she'd written the invitation herself.

I had no choice then but to hand the card over. She held it out at arm's length, like a menu; she was getting farsighted and didn't have her reading glasses on. She let out a small, involuntary sound when she came to Katherine's postscript, then stopped short at the look on my face. She raised the card to her forehead and squinted out underneath it to some distant point of the horizon. "The party isn't till June. Maybe you'll be feeling better by then."

"Maybe," I said. I didn't say that I wasn't going either way.

"Let us hope." She opened the sack I'd tossed onto the porch and peered inside. "Oh Willie," she said. "Must you smoke? Don't you read the medical reports?"

I glanced meaningfully at the pitcher of vodka in front of her.

She registered my disapproval and moved on. "That poor girl. Just imagine having that tragic home life to contend with . . ."

I sensed Malachi's touch again. "*What* tragic home life?" I asked.

"Doesn't she say Malachi will be there, too?"

"What's he got to do with anything?" I said.

"I just don't want you getting dragged into something over your head."

"What are you talking about?" I asked. "Dragged in how?"

"Never mind. I suppose it's for the best." She had on her mysterious, tea-leaf-reading look, a face that drove me crazy.

I bent to pick up my cigarettes and the newspaper and saw the street behind me upside down. The pavement was shimmering, vibrating in the heat. Like the first explosive drops of a storm, there was a scattering of notes at the back of my head.

"Oh Willie, Willie." For one hideous second I thought my mother was going to cry. I'd have done anything to prevent that. Instead she looked away. She blinked rapidly and pushed her fingers through her hair. "*Must* you smoke?" she asked again. "It's so bad for you."

"Cheer up," I said. "I'm six foot one. Tobacco can no longer stunt my growth."

"You're driving us into an early grave," she warned.

I smiled unhappily. "It's too late even for that," I said.

Chapter Two

MALACHI GELB was the kind of unassimilated, old-style, Old Testament Jew despised by people of all religions, but especially his own. His name was peculiar; he had no manners, no sense of diplomacy; in an age of immaculate hygiene he sometimes smelled sweaty and sour. He had flaming red hair and the pale, freckled, ghastly-looking skin to go with it, a smile that hooked up at the sides like a sarcastic trout. *Homely* was too mild a word to describe him; Malachi was anything but mild.

I first got to know Malachi in orchestra class, my sophomore year at school, but I'd seen him around before then—he was hard to miss. He'd stand at the door to the student lobby, glaring at the rest of us like a newly arrived immigrant, shifting his weight from one leg to the other, his skinny arms folded across his chest for protection. He sported a Communist Chinese cap with a red star on its front, and a knitted green wool scarf around his neck regardless of the season: He was a political scientist, and music was just a hobby, though he played passable violin, cello, and bass viol. It didn't matter what he took, he was always at the top of our class. By his junior year he'd already been accepted, early admission, to Columbia. The only way to rattle him was to say his name repeatedly as you spoke—Malachi, Malachi, Malachi—that got to him, and no one had ever been kind enough to endow him with a nickname.

At dinner he'd wait till the other music students had left my table and I had taken out some scores to study, his face long and dour as he clicked his tray against mine. He had a hard time finding someplace to eat because he kept a strictly kosher diet. If as a joke someone tossed a sandwich onto his plate, he'd throw the whole meal away as polluted, get a new tray, and start over again on line. By the time he got back, someone else would usually be at his place. I suppose I felt sorry for him. He wasn't exactly a popular dinner companion.

We lived in the same coed dormitory at school, a building unofficially reserved for musicians; boys and girls in different wings on the same floor. He played various stringed instruments for the school orchestra: cello, bass, whatever was needed. Sometimes he sat next to me, second cello to my first. That was how we'd started talking.

"Hey—Steinberg. Mind if I sit here?" he'd ask at dinner, making a sweeping gesture with his one free hand and hanging on to his tray with the other. Since I didn't know how to get rid of him politely and suffered in those days from an exaggerated sense of noblesse oblige, we ended up eating meals together a few nights a week—or rather, he ate while I studied my music, usually in silence. Once in a while he'd break in on my train of thought to catalog my faults, a long list of them, drumming his fingers on the tabletop and staring at me. There was a morbid fascination to these conversations.

"Listen, Steinberg," he'd say. "A little criticism never hurt anyone." He'd make a tent out of his two hands and frame me with the triangle, squinting as if he didn't like what he saw. "You know I don't tell you these things gratuitously. You've got more problems than you know. Believe me, I'm not the only one who sees it. People talk. You think you're Jehovah, but on the seventh day at least He rested. Plus, you're a prude. What's up with you?"

I'd study the score held up in front of my face. Once in a while I'd grunt or try to change the subject. "Flute triple fortissimo— ridiculous but interesting."

I barely tolerated Malachi, but this other girl, Katherine Randolph, befriended him. Her father belonged to the Country Club of Virginia, and she had been schooled till her sophomore year at St. Catherine's School for Girls in Richmond, as had her mother, her grandmother, and great-grandmother before her. I think she'd gotten into some kind of trouble there, though nobody knew what kind or why. Malachi maintained that her mother, like the jealous queen in "Snow White," just wanted her out of the way.

Katherine was closemouthed to the point of feigning muteness, with big gray eyes that had a disconcertingly deadpan expression. I never heard her talk about anything remotely interesting—her passion seemed to be vintage designer clothing. But she had perfect pitch and the only first-rate alto voice I'd ever heard in someone my own age, the kind of voice that carried across the bleachers, pure and steady on. When she dropped out of the high school choir halfway through her first semester, she left a hole in the alto section that never was filled. No one else even came close. She didn't seem to care much about it, the gift she had. That was what amazed me.

She always looked unhealthy in the faintly decadent way of one of the Rossettis from the end of the nineteenth century. She had puffy, dark circles under her eyes, which came from pernicious anemia, Malachi said—a disease I'd never heard of anyone having north of the Mason-Dixon line. Malachi assured me it would kill her sooner or later. But he also hinted that Mr. Randolph, her father—bulwark of the Southern Commonwealth Stock Exchange—was a chronic drunk and a Seventh-Day Adventist who moonlighted in a

Richmond hotel on weekends. Malachi was unreliable about everything having to do with Katherine because he was in love with her. I'd never been in love, and if Malachi was any example, I didn't ever want to be. I went out casually with other musicians—horn players or fellow cellists; serious-minded young men who dressed even worse than the art students, walking around all winter in floppy rubber sandals and Bermuda shorts.

Katherine was as out of place in our world as an antimacassar. She and Malachi cut a crazy figure together, walking across the Commons lawn—Katherine in one of her good gray wool suits, a black hat tilted back on her bright reddish gold hair; Malachi just a step or two behind, as if to keep her from running away. He followed her in his beat-up Chevy van and carried a copy of her class schedule in his pocket. He'd take out the worn-out scrap of paper and show it to me sometimes, as if it was a difficult score that maybe I could explicate. Once he even bought three column inches in the *Philadelphia Inquirer*, announcing their engagement on the family page. She took all of this in undismayed, which made me wonder what exactly was wrong with her.

Katherine sweetened his bitterness; he could not put out her light, though he must have tried—it was in his nature. He was a storm brewer, a courter of tragedy. His mother—a survivor, as he liked to brag, of Auschwitz and Bergen-Belsen—had died of mysterious complications when he was a kid, and everyone knew that he despised his father. He should have lived at home; instead he boarded with the out-of-state students.

Mr. Gelb was a lawyer in downtown Philadelphia, maybe half a mile away from campus. He brought his black alligator briefcase with him whenever he visited Malachi at the high school, as if he'd come to consult a client. Malachi liked to hint at unsavory motives behind the visits, trips away from the downtown office. "A little something on the back burner," he'd sneer. "A college girl, maybe —I hear he likes them young."

When Mr. Gelb showed up, he always wore the same type of expensive, charcoal gray business suit, in a shiny material that made the creases look like they'd been cut with a knife. It was impossible to imagine him in anything less sharp, more casual—without that expensive leather attaché, white shirt, and tie. I had the feeling Mr. Gelb himself would have felt lost without them.

Apart from their matching sarcastic smiles, Malachi and his father didn't even look related. Mr. Gelb was dark-skinned and handsome, in a sardonic, Sephardic way; Malachi was pure Georgia Russian Jew. He took after the redheaded girl who peered accusingly out of an antique wedding frame displayed shrinelike on the floor of his room. This was Mr. Gelb's first wife, Malachi's mother. She looked antique herself, with glowingly retouched teeth and pearls, her lips painted pink as a corpse's. Time had left her stranded there on the floor.

Mr. Gelb, her former husband, was a thoroughly contemporary man. His voice was soft and nasal, his laughter coarse. He spoke to his son in a sly, confidential way that didn't inspire confidence, tapping him lightly, insistently on the arm as he talked. Together they would pace the dormitory hall arguing, shoulder to shoulder, their faces turned away from each other like a two-headed god.

"The man is a tyrant!" Malachi would announce loudly as soon as his father had left. "A tyrant!"

A few months before I dropped out of school, I happened upon a scene between the father and son. Most of the resident student body had gone home for the winter break; the commuters had all fled, but I'd stayed on a few extra days for the civic orchestra's Christmas concert. My father had written to say that he wouldn't make it home for the holidays again that year, and my mother had flown up to New York to visit a cousin. I was to meet her there, then we'd go on down to Richmond together. School seemed especially peaceful right then, like a half-empty train I was riding alone. I was working on a tour-de-force composition, an octet for strings and wind.

The last homebound stragglers had been wandering around the halls all day, typing up final exams, dragging suitcases, while car horns blared outside and doors slammed up and down the corridors. The unlucky few who'd stayed behind were eating the school cafeteria's nonfestive turkey with canned cranberry sauce.

I'd gone out with a few of the civic players for supper in downtown Philadelphia, then walked back from the central office, where the second cellist, a small-claims lawyer, dropped me off at the curb. As the only high-school-age student in the orchestra, I was petted and admired, praised no matter how I played. My snow-flecked cello case banged rhythmically against my knee as I thought over the music we'd heard straight through for the first time that night in dress rehearsal.

It was Beethoven's *Missa Solemnus,* a long score seldom performed in full. The piece is too peculiar to be a crowd-pleaser, and too melancholy. His angelic voices are full of misgivings, the orchestra oceanic but lost, like a whale out of water. Beethoven himself comes across as thoughtful and remote in a way that troubles audiences, and was bothering me, too. Trying to come to terms with the music was like trying to reconstruct a cathedral I'd walked through only once.

I was grateful for the company of the other musicians after rehearsal, adults with jobs and preoccupations, for whom music was just a pleasant diversion. I liked listening to them while we stood outside during breaks and on the ride home in the backseat of the lawyer's big convertible with the cello resting across my lap, watching the early winter dusk descending around us like a minor scale. It had snowed for the second time that week, and the Christmas lights strung on houses threw scattered reflections on the snow-filmed lawns.

It was a cold walk from the central office back to the dorm, and my feet were numb by the time I got there, but I was content. I wasn't worrying about my father's not coming home or my mother's emotional state. The only thing on my mind was the music we had just played that night in rehearsal. I shoved open the dormitory door with my shoulder and made my way up two flights of stairs, replaying in my head the closing of the *Agnus Dei*, where everything massive and Germanic that has gone before begins to dissolve, transforms itself into an airy Jacob's ladder. "From the heart," Beethoven wrote at the top of the score, "may it go to the heart!" As I rounded the last bend in the dimly lit staircase I heard shouting—or maybe it came into focus just then, like real voices invading a dream. I stopped and switched the cello case from one hand to the other, blinking snow out of my eyes.

One of two figures was hunched over, as if with a stomachache. I stopped in my tracks.

His red hair looked coppery under the hall lamp. He stuck one skinny arm into the air, pointing a finger. "I won't be spit on! I don't like to be spit on!" Malachi's voice was shrill. He stood facing his father. "Go on—go home! I wouldn't be caught dead in your miserable house, with that shiksa waving a wooden spoon in my face. An all-American family like that, I'm sure you must be very proud of yourself—believe me, I sympathize and I wouldn't want to interfere with your domestic bliss!" I tried to find another way out—they were blocking the only route back to my room.

Mr. Gelb stood slouched under the hall lamp. His smile looked bored. "I was just offering you a small vacation," he said calmly, jingling change in his pants pocket. "Don't have a heart attack."

"I know what you were offering," Malachi said loudly. "But I'll have to decline! I *hate* skiing—it's a fascistic, disgusting, bourgeois sport, and last year I spent two full days in the freezing cold infirmary before I could even get hold of you. Two full days! The night nurse brought me a cup of ginger ale; she told me, 'Pretend it's champagne.' I was on some kind of drugs to kill the pain—maybe you remember—so we toasted each other's health. It was all very cheerful, a fine New Year's Eve, I had a wonderful time!" His voice rose a few notes. "Thanks very much! You've made your great offer, you can go home now. Go with an easy conscience, Pop. Buy your wife and kids some Tupperware with the money you'll save. Tell them it's a Christmas present from your son the Jew! Just spare me, please, this mockery of a father's concern!"

Mr. Gelb took his hands out of his pockets. "Now you listen to me, Malachi—"

"No!" Malachi's hands rose slowly in the air, then fell back to his sides. "For eighteen years I've been listening. I've been paying very close attention. If you want to take care of me, take care of me. If not, not.— Just don't pretend!" He wheeled around in the hall, his coat ballooning—a sprig of holly sprucing up his lapel—and strode away toward the men's wing. He slammed his door hard, a sound that echoed through the almost empty corridor.

I set down my cello to ease my hand, and the floorboards creaked. Mr. Gelb swiveled around to stare at me. I flexed my hand and picked up the cello, feeling gawky and funereal in my long black recital dress. I sidled past Mr. Gelb and the bulky, rope-tied suitcase Malachi had left out in the hall. Mr. Gelb pretended not to see me. I returned the favor, fumbling with my papers and keys. I slipped into my dorm room, lugging the cello in one hand, the orchestra folder under my arm, and shut the door behind me with my foot. All of the music had vanished from my head.

Later that night—at 3:17 A.M. by the digital clock next to my bed—I heard a long, thin cry floating down the hall. Half dreaming, I thought it must be the dorm cat stuck between some icy window ledge and a tree. Our high school had a rule against pets, but someone was always sneaking one in. The sound came again, then lower pitched, distinctly human, and suddenly I was awake and scared, sitting up in bed. I fumbled some clothing out of my suitcase, stuck my feet into a pair of sneakers, and stumbled down the hall toward the men's section of the dorm.

"Hello?" I called. "Is everything okay?"

The dormitory was still, like a becalmed ship. I had the impression that below the building lay a dark body of water. I moved close to a window and saw snow sifting down toward the ground, settling over the lampposts like a veil. One lone student, head lowered against the snow—male or female, you couldn't tell which from the bundled-up figure—glided into the dormitory next door. I slumped back against the wall and tied my shoelaces. The dismal sound came again. I recognized the voice. The cry contained so much undisguised human suffering that I was afraid to be alone with it. The vibrations echoed in the hall for a second.

I took a few more steps, this time toward Malachi's room, one hand out in front of me in the air as if holding away cobwebs, then lost courage at the last second and hurried down two flights of stairs and straight out the door. The snow rose up around my ankles, waking me instantly.

The all-women's dormitory next door had neatly spray-painted stars and snowflakes decorating the black window glass. Their building always looked more like an elementary school than ours. Two floors up, someone's Christmas lights were still on—a double row of pale violet lights in the flat, even outline of a heart. I had seen Malachi a dozen times standing under Katherine Randolph's room like a serenading Romeo. The more I considered it, moving around underneath to check the angles—the more I thought it was the window with the purple lights. I scooped up a handful of snow and stood alone in the bitter cold, aimlessly packing and shaping the snow with my bare hands. The room was dark behind the violet heart. I took aim without thinking and let fly, aiming the snowball at the dead center of the lights. My pitch was just a little high and to the side. The room lights instantly snapped on, amber against the shade, as if I'd hit a switch. Then someone raised the shade. I ducked back, but it was too late to hide. Katherine slid open the window and stuck her head out.

"What time is it?" she asked calmly, as if she were used to being called on in this way.

"It's Grace Steinberg," I said. "You know—Steinberg. We were in chorus together once. Can you come down? There's some kind of trouble in Malachi's room."

"What sort of trouble?"

"I'm not positive," I said. "Noises."

"Noises?" she said. "You're the girl who writes all the music, aren't you? Didn't you win that G.E. award last year?"

I'd forgotten to put socks on, and my ankles were burning from the cold. I kicked one sneaker sideways against the other. "I guess. Would you mind if we discussed this inside? I'm kind of chilly."

"Of course not!" She seemed embarrassed, which suddenly accentuated her Southern drawl. "Come on up, Grace. My room's right at the top of the stairs." She said it "rot at the top of the stars."

"Okay," I told her. "But my name isn't—" Too late. She had already pulled her head back inside and closed the window.

Inside, the all-women dormitories were identical to ours, except the walls were tinted a pale peachy color instead of mint green, and there was a stale flowery smell of shampoo left over in the halls.

Katherine stood at the door to her room, blinking and buttoning the cuff of a delicate-looking white blouse. There was a name-

tag beside her door, printed in boldface:
Katherine Bolton Randolph. I felt as if I
ought to ring a doorbell and greet the maid.

"Won't you come in?" she asked. Her
greeting reminded me of the servant I'd been
expecting, and the room itself added to the
effect. I realized this was because it was wall-
papered, in dark blue paper with yellow
roses. I'd never seen that sort of thing before.

"I'll just grab a few things," she said.
"Would you care to sit down while you wait?"

"Thanks," I said, but I stayed standing.
"We'd better get going." There were stacks of
small, expensive-looking clothing all over the
room—piled on the bed, on her desk, filling
an armchair by the window. I couldn't have
found a place to sit down if I'd tried. She must
have been packing earlier—or else holding a
rummage sale. Other than the few pieces of
furniture covered with clothing, the room was
empty, studded with a few peculiar-looking
objects. It made the place seem desolate, like
an auction house after the auction. A pair of
navy blue cups stood alone on the floor. Katherine saw me look at them.

"Those are silver-chased coconut cups,"

she said. "They belonged to my great-aunt Mary." She pronounced *aunt* so it rhymed with *haunt*.

The cups didn't look like coconuts to me, but I nodded.

"Would you care for a Diet Pepsi?" she asked.

"No thanks. You live here alone?" I pitied her roommate.

She nodded, touching a barrette in her hair. "She transferred out this fall." She picked up a huge black canvas bag, walked to the window, and turned off the heart. Her face was cast partly in shadow, cut neatly in half, and for a second she reminded me of someone, but I couldn't think who. There was an electric clock by the bed, but it wasn't plugged in. She tossed a silver-handled hairbrush into the bag, and two pill bottles. Then she walked into her closet, stepping over more piles of clothing. Her voice echoed back. "I'll be right with you. Are you sure you wouldn't care for a D.P.?"

"I'm sure. We'd really better get going." I had tracked in clumps of snow and now they were melting in slow muddy rivulets toward her pale-colored cashmere sweaters and silk scarves. I shuffled my sneakers around, trying to redistribute the puddles, but I was too tired to keep it up. I figured it must be almost four o'clock in the morning. "Don't you have a working clock?" I asked.

Katherine emerged from the closet holding a silky beige nightgown in one hand. "No. It's probably close to midnight, wouldn't you think? I'll be right back." She padded barefoot across the room, into my snow puddles and out again, over piles of blouses into the hall, leaving shiny footprints across the wood floor.

I walked over to the pale violet heart. At the window hung rich-looking gold-and-rose-flowered curtains that matched the wallpaper. The bed was covered with pastel sweaters, skirts, and blouses, all in tiny sizes. I felt like one of those giants in trick photographs whose heads brush the ceiling. I paced nervously by the door, then back to the window, pulling the shade aside. It was snowing again, falling straight and fine like a child's hair.

Katherine appeared in the doorway, still barefoot, wearing glasses. The glasses made her look younger, more vulnerable. "I guess I'm ready," she said.

"Okay. But you'll need shoes," I told her. "It's snowing."

She opened her closet door and pulled out a tattered fur coat, which she put on. She slid her feet into a pair of high-heeled red summer sandals. I stared at them.

"Something wrong?" she asked.

"No, I guess. Let's go."

I followed her down the stairs and outside. She sank nearly to her bare shins, wobbling in the snow.

"Do you want to go back and change shoes?" I asked.

"Why?" she said calmly. "We're just going next door."

The sky had turned the murky color it does before dawn. Flakes of snow were coming down thick and fast, blinking on the sleeves of her fur coat. She lifted her feet carefully, like a dancer. "Malachi is a very unusual person," she said.

I plowed on ahead of her. "Yeah. He's crazy."

We entered my building on the women's side. A small yellow lamp bracketed to the wall cast a wooden glow over everything. The hall was quiet. "The boys' dorm rooms are that way," I said, pointing ahead.

Katherine was holding her glasses in one hand, looking at them as if they were fossils she had just uncovered. She breathed on the lenses one at a time, wiping them clean on the sleeve of her coat. "I know where they are," she said.

Wind beat at the windows, rattling the glass. A radiator banged twice and hissed to itself. Then it was quiet again; I could almost hear the snow outside piling against itself. There was a loud crash down the hall. I jumped and Katherine grabbed my arm. The crash was followed by a glassy tinkling sound, then steady pounding, like someone bouncing a basketball.

"I'd better go," Katherine whispered. "It sounds like he's hitting his head on the wall."

A door swung open in front of us, revealing a sleepy-looking senior, his belly hanging over his jockey shorts like a middle-aged man's, his face puffy with sleep. "Will you tell that moron to quiet down? I've got an early bus to catch."

"Please close your door," Katherine said quietly.

He opened his mouth to answer, staring first at her, then at me.

"Sweet dreams," she said.

The boy's lips compressed. He smirked uneasily. The door swung slowly shut in our faces. From behind it came a long whistle.

Katherine smoothed back her hair. She stood there in the hall, flat-footed on her clunky red sandals. For that second she reminded me again of someone, but before I could think who she turned away.

"Good night," she said. "Get some sleep, Grace."

"My name's really Willie."

"Okay—Willie. Thanks for coming to get me."

When she had clutched at my arm, I'd been startled at the texture of her coat sleeve. Dull gray, tipped with silver—it was an old mink, I realized, an expensive one. Light glinted on the safety pin that held one side of her glasses together. I knew who she reminded me of, then.

"It's nothing," I said. "Good night." For reasons I couldn't begin to understand, I envied her her place in the world. Watching her from the back, when she walked away from me—her spine so erect and her hair glittering red, patient as a servant yet stubbornly her own woman—she looked a lot like my mother.

The next morning I visited Malachi's room. Out in the hall I could hear him clicking rapidly away on his electric typewriter. There was no answer when I knocked. He didn't even look up when I pushed the door open, but he slid the paper out and shut the machine off, keeping his profile to me. A muscle jumped at the side of his jaw, and he clamped his fingers over it.

"So, how are you feeling?" I asked.

"How am I *feeling?*" he repeated, mockingly. "I *feel fine,* thank you."

"Maybe I'll come back—"

"Sit," he said, with a rough gesture.

The room was sterile and orderly, filled with an impressive array of stainless steel machinery: typewriter, TV, a white-noise machine that roared like the ocean. He had an expensive Bang & Olufsen stereo setup I'd never even heard him play. Every object in the room looked sterilized, except for the antique portrait of his mother. Sharp morning light poured in through his unshaded window.

He reached for a cigarette, lit it, and went into a coughing fit. I moved toward him. "I'm fine!" he snapped, holding up one hand. "Don't mother me!"

"Okay," I said irritably. "Choke to death."

"Next time leave me alone," he said. "I don't appreciate your nosing around like some spook house detective in a third-rate hotel. I mean it! Just leave me alone."

"Believe me, I will."

"What did you come by for?" he asked. "Cheap thrills? You want to snoop under the bed? See if there are any women there, any broken needles?"

"Why don't you go to hell?" I opened his door.

"Wait, Steinberg. Stop." He sprang to his feet and leaned against the desk. He stared at the floor. "Sorry. I appreciate your concern."

"Forget it," I said. "I'm glad you're all right."

He half turned away from me, toward the window. I didn't know what else to say. I ran through one or two platitudes and rejected them. I stared around at his walls as if some-

thing better might be written there. He
reached forward with one hand and switched
on the typewriter. Its soft humming filled the
room. He flicked it off. " 'And he shall turn
the hearts of the children to the fathers, and
the fathers to the children, lest I come and
smite the earth with a curse.' " He stared at
his desktop. "It's all darkness out there,
Steinberg. You know what I'm talking about.
Don't you. That's why we're both so—"

"You just need rest," I said. "That's all."

"Right." He stared at his hand lying palm
down on the desk. He opened and closed his
fingers. He had big hands, like an adult's.
"I'd rather be dead in Gehenna," he said
thoughtfully, still studying and flexing his
hand. "All things considered. There at least
I'd have the company of the other lost souls."

"Have a nice Christmas," I said, and
yanked open the door and didn't slow down
or look back till I'd reached the safety of my
own room.

Chapter Three

IN JUNE THE first wave of true summer heat sank down on the city of Richmond and would not budge. You couldn't escape that kind of temperature or get used to it; you just learned to live with it as if you'd suddenly grown an extra limb and had to drag it around with you.

Our house on Gardenia had two small air conditioners—one in my mother's bedroom, one in the kitchen—and a rusty attic fan that stirred up the hot, humid air in the rest of the house with a lonely, whirring sound like crickets. I had a prudish aversion to spending time in anyone else's bedroom, so I sat downstairs at the kitchen table, with my hair pinned up and the back of my neck practically touching the vents of the air conditioner.

We ate our meals in the kitchen or sometimes, with forced, sweaty festivity, on the screened-in side porch, where we'd pretend it felt a few degrees cooler in the shade. At night, bats somehow got in to the upstairs bedrooms and flapped around from wall to wall, like creatures from outer space. My mother stood out in the hall, her laughter hysterical, while I threw towels over the homely animals one by one and flung them out the window onto the lawn below, where, I imagined, they shook off their leathery wings and waited for the next good opportunity to fly back in.

I'd driven up to school for final exams at the end of May. I'd only gotten my driver's license a few months earlier, so the act of driving a car long-distance still felt fresh and faintly terrifying. The trees were in full leaf, and the Commons lawn looked like a bowling green. I managed to squeak by in every class except Diatonic Composition, which I flunked by scrawling something unflattering to contemporary theory at the bottom of the final exam. I had to have a conversation with the dean about it before I left, along with some general talk about my future. He had dug up a few college application forms and told me if I got them filled out by the fall, there was no reason I couldn't start college in the middle of that next year. I did a lot of nodding in his office and then kept nodding while I walked all the way around the grounds, under the green broad-leafed trees, in and out of every building I had ever visited, trying to drum up some final feeling of farewell. Instead it backfired. Standing at the edge of the Commons lawn, watching the younger students rushing around, their arms still loaded down with books, I felt like a ghostly stranger in the middle of my own turf, as if I'd never really been there at all. The feeling of not belonging was so acute I thought I must be actually, literally invisible. It startled me when one of my teachers greeted me in the music hall.

Driving back into Richmond was almost a relief, because the heat was so physical and all-absorbing: like leaning face first into the open door of an oven. My breath locked up inside my chest, and all my movements turned heavy and slow, as if I'd been dropped under water.

In the few days I'd been away, the music room had mysteriously turned back into my father's study—my mother had been in there moving furniture around, putting back his things. One morning I found a pair of his sunglasses in a drawer, brittle and frail as the skeleton of a small animal. I buried them in the bottom of a trash basket.

Because of the tall French windows facing south, that study was the hottest room in the house. I set a rotating fan on top of the Baldwin, and whenever I wasn't watching closely, the music paper would rise up piece by piece and flap around the room. I held my hands on the slippery keys, back to work again, viciously scratching "Symphony Number One" at the top of every page. It seemed like my only hope. I had talked my teacher into giving me an Incomplete for the senior thesis, and I was determined to finish it before the fall.

Blue flies buzzed against the sun-filled windows, bumping into the glass like coins, and their slow death rattle, confused with the whirring fan and resonant dry ticking of the metronome, made it impossible for me to think. My mother had begun making a few friends in the neighborhood, so now there was sometimes the sound of their high-pitched chattering and fitful laughter from the porch or living room.

After I'd crumpled up every page I'd written—carefully and methodically, as if I thought the CIA might be interested—I'd collapse into a yellow damask armchair next to my cello and sit staring at the wallpaper or out at the basketball hoop, wiping sweat from the back of my neck. My grandfather's music libary was still in there, so I reread the lives of the German composers in volumes so old the gilt edges had rubbed away. I paid particular, close attention to the letters Mozart had written, trapped in his city of Salzburg, and studied every word he had ever written in English, as if his use of my native language might convey some special message: *Please don't never forget your dear friend Mozart.*

Neighboring children played decorous games of tag under the broad, thick-leaved trees; the girls wearing starched cotton dresses, the boys in military-style shorts and short-sleeved shirts. Sometimes they set up sprinklers on the lawns and marched back and forth through the dazzling arch.

My mother delivered glasses of iced tea

outside my study door. That was our chief form of communication during the day. The only proof of her bodily presence was the clinking of ice cubes as she put down the tray, like the Beast serving Beauty—or, more accurately, like Beauty serving the Beast. I could hear her pacing up and down the upstairs hall next to the telephone or running the vacuum cleaner over and over the same narrow path, shutting off the motor now and then as if she thought she'd heard the phone ringing. She'd climb up and down the stairs two or three times a day to check the mail, creaking the lid of the letter box open and closed, and I always knew when the mail had arrived because her footsteps were slower and heavier heading back upstairs.

She turned forty in early June, and my father sent a card with pink roses on the front. We celebrated at home, the two of us, with a birthday cake after supper, one I had baked in the middle of the night while the house felt almost cool. After supper I carried the dishes into the kitchen and washed and dried them. I'd bought her a pair of earrings and a dozen white carnations because they were her favorite flower and a funny card that on second thought didn't seem so funny, but I'd already signed it. She put a lot of effort into acting jolly and pleased, tried on the new earrings, and went to bed early. I sat up a long time after she'd gone upstairs, reading magazines but mostly just turning pages. When the phone finally rang, I picked up on the first ring.

It was my father; a little drunk, I could tell, because when he'd been drinking his voice always got higher and tighter, more excited, and he'd wax so sentimental it made my skin crawl. I hadn't talked to him in over a month.

That night he went on about wanting to buy me a Porsche, now that he was making some real money. He was going to buy it just as soon as the car dealers opened in the morning and wanted to know what color did I want. Silver? Red?

I mentioned a blouse I had seen in one of the Richmond department stores. "Mom would like it," I said. "It's her birthday. Remember? Should I go get her?"

"I know it is," he said after a second. "Sure. Put her on."

My mother wandered downstairs a long while later, her face so stupidly radiant I wanted to throw something at her. Now *she'd* be sitting around waiting for a Porsche, the way she'd been waiting for the mail. She had put on a flowered dress with ruffles, as if she'd gone to a party for her birthday instead of to bed early and alone.

She took a swizzle stick and a pink paper napkin from the cupboard and made herself a lemonade and vodka. She offered me one, too, but I said I wasn't old enough to drink—and anyway I didn't believe in drinking, unlike some people I knew.

"I see," she said, more amused than upset. While she was standing with her back to me at the counter, she mentioned that she was planning a trip to southwest Africa in August. The blue-bordered pamphlet had risen to the top of that particular pile and stayed there.

"August is Africa's loveliest time of year," she added. "It rains a lot, but it's very cool and fresh—like autumn in New England."

"So why not wait a month and go to New England?" I said.

She turned and gave me a sharp look, one

hand flat on the counter. "Your father will love it. We can buy the safari outfits when we get there."

"Oh," I said. "Is he going?"

"Did you think I was going to Africa alone?"

I stared at the brochure, turning it toward me so I wouldn't have to look at her. I'll never be like her, I promised myself. "When are you leaving?"

"It's not altogether definite." She stirred her drink with the striped swizzle stick, then shook it and set it down on the paper napkin. "I may as well wait till your father comes home." She hunched her shoulders to sip her drink and peeked at me over the rim of her glass. "He'll be getting his summer vacation soon."

"Uh-huh." In a normal house this would have been a normal conversation. I listened to the kitchen clock *tsk-tsk*ing over her head and nodded. She didn't take her eyes from my face. I pursed my lips thoughtfully and nodded again.

"How about them Yankees?" I said, after a while. "You think they've got a chance at the pennant?" She didn't answer, and after a few more seconds, I picked up my glass of iced tea and retreated into the study.

I kept back issues of *Musical America* in there, and I sat in the armchair, sipping iced tea and turning pages. Hopeless, hopeless. It was already too hot to draw a breath, and it wasn't even light out. A car went by, tires hissing on the asphalt, so I knew it had rained again. The car turned the corner, its headlights bouncing around the room. It lit up one of my father's old sports trophies on the mantel, a relic I had somehow overlooked. I felt the blood beating at my temples, in time to the rosewood metronome ticking on top of the Baldwin. *Here, gone. Here, gone.* After a few more seconds of that I got up from my chair, my shirtdress clinging to the backs of my legs, and shut the damned thing off and faced it to the wall.

The next morning the phone woke me. I startled upright, anxious, scared that it was my father again, still drunk, or more drunk, or the state police calling about him from the side of a ditch.

"Willie. Is that you?" The voice at the other end was female, Southern, and breathlessly polite, like all of my mother's new friends. She said something else I couldn't hear over a clattering of dishes.

"Yes," I said. "May I tell her who's calling?"

"It's Katherine Randolph, how are *you?*"

"Oh, I'm fine," I said, trying to sound like I was awake, or at least conscious. "Is anything wrong?" I asked.

"No . . . I was just wondering." She hesitated; her voice almost audibly hovered. "Did you get my invitation?"

"Oh—yes, I did. Thanks!"

There was a short silence. "Are you coming?"

"Oh. Coming? Didn't you get my note?" Of course she hadn't, but I was planning to send my regrets as soon as I had the chance. One of these days. The only thing certain was that I wasn't going. Anywhere. I dragged the phone back into my room and sank down on the bed, rubbing one hand through my hair. Light slanted on the coverlet. I had no idea what time it was.

She said, "I need to ask you something. Is that all right?"

"Sure," I said. "Go ahead."

"Do you think you could come by?"

"Come by to your house, do you mean?"

"Well, yes," she said. "Around two?"

"What for?" I asked.

Someone picked up on the line. I could hear the echo of our radio playing downstairs. We both waited. "Mama?" Katherine asked. "Is that you?" The phone clicked again.

"I'm sorry," Katherine said. "She does that sometimes." There was a mutually embarrassed silence. "You know where I live, don't you? It's a mauve-colored house on Carey. Number four. There are so many black cars in the driveway it looks like we're having a funeral. Will two o'clock suit you?"

"Yes," I found myself saying. "A mauve house?"

"That's right. Thank you." She sounded genuinely grateful.

"I'm sorry if I woke you, Willie."

"No, that's okay." I hung up and nearly went straight back to bed, but something made me pick up the clock from my night table. It was already one-thirty in the afternoon. My heart plummeted—if I'd had the courage I'd have called back and canceled. It had been a long time since I'd been in any kind of a social setting at all. Listening to one neighbor's music through the open window and nodding to another on the front lawn was about it. I wrote down "Number 4 Carey— mauve house" on a scrap of paper and shoved it in the pocket of my shorts. Still, it felt good to have somewhere to go.

"Where are you running off to?" my mother asked as I came through the kitchen. She was at the table, underlining passages from the African travel brochure, highlighting words with a yellow Magic Marker. There were exclamation points and question marks all over the margins; it looked like the decoding of some ancient language. A new catalog from Bennington College had been added to the pile at my end of the table.

She smiled at me brilliantly, pushing the blond hair back from her forehead. "The mail came early."

"That's good." I made a halfhearted perusal of the college catalog cover. It looked like the front of a *Vermont Life* calendar.

"Your father sent another card," she said. "Would you like to see it?"

"Maybe later." I had stopped reading his postcards months earlier.

"It's right on the table in the hall if you change your mind. It's an especially nice one."

An especially nice one, I thought. I'll bet. Still, I detoured at the last second and went to the table in the foyer. I picked the postcard up and looked at it blankly. It showed the front of some anonymous-looking chain hotel with a numbing quantity of small square windows, all of them lit up yellow. There wasn't anything nice about it. My mother was crazy. I ran my thumb over the slick, grainy surface of the postcard, put it back down on the table unread. Then I wiped my hands on the sides of my dress and left by way of the side porch.

Katherine was standing framed by her front door; she waved me into the driveway as I approached, as if afraid I might drive past. I would have, too, if I'd been watching for a mauve house. Hers was made of stone the greenish gray color of old moss, between other old houses with lawns as long and well tended as bowling greens. I got out of my car and closed the door behind me, feeling clumsy and eight feet tall. Insects buzzed shrilly in the heat, and my dress was already damp against my back. The Randolphs' house was as tall and narrow as the Episcopalian church a few houses away. Katherine waved again and watched me walk the long way around, down the driveway and up the front path, avoiding the neatly manicured front lawn.

"Willie! How nice to see you," she said loudly as I came to the door. She smelled of a kind of violet perfume I associated with old ladies. "How have you been?" She leaned forward and opened the screen door, pulling it from behind. I stepped into the foyer, trying to adjust my eyes to the sudden gloom. "It's so good of you to come!" It sounded as if she were speaking to someone one or two rooms away.

As if in response, a woman's voice rose in tired agitation. "Katherine? Who's at the door?"

"Please wait," Katherine hissed at me, ducking her head. "That's my mother. I'll be right back."

I was left standing alone in the tiny dim foyer. To my right, taking up most of one wall, hung a huge oil painting of a girl picking flowers in a field. The girl looked familiar, and I took a step back to see her whole. She stared back with dull, unhappy eyes. A bluish black vapor curled around her bare feet, the strands of fog congealing into the suggestion of human features, a leer. At the bottom of the frame was a title plaque: *Death and the Maiden*. I stepped back violently, said "Excuse me!" to the wall behind me, and hurried out under the archway through which my hostess had disappeared.

Out in the larger hall hung smaller paintings, gallery-style portraits with discreet old-fashioned lights in metal hoods above each. Katherine came toward me, her arms folded like a nun's. "That's my uncle, Calder Eppes." She nodded at the opposite wall, to the row of portraits. "That's my father's twin sister, Margaret Day, and their cousins. That one back there"—she waved back to the dark foyer—"my mother modeled for when she was a child. It's neoclassical LeBourget—he was an eminent Southern painter of the twenties and thirties. Most of the pictures along this wall are new. We don't care for them much. Would you like to say hello to my mother? She's been dying to meet you. You're looking well," she said. That was surely a lie. "Are you feeling better?"

"I feel fine," I said. I suppose I thought if I said it often enough there was a chance it would come true.

We walked together down a corridor and into a large bedroom with the shades drawn tight. In full sun it would have been all white, like a hospital room. A pungent, sharp-sweet alcohol smell greeted us as we crossed the threshold.

"That's witch hazel," Katherine whispered. "My mother uses it for her eyes."

"Please don't whisper." Mrs. Randolph lay on top of the bedclothes, looking up at the ceiling. Her dress was so voluminous, she seemed to levitate there. It was something flounced and blue, which I think my mother would have called a cocktail dress. Her reddish gold hair was spread in a lion's mane on the pillow. "I always know you're talking about me when you whisper. So thrilled to meet you," she added my way.

"How do you do," I said.

"Not very well, dear." Mrs. Randolph shifted her body a little. "Hasn't your father come in yet, Katherine? I thought I heard voices."

"Mama, this is Grace—Willie—my

friend from up at school. The musician, you remember."

"Oh, of course." She rolled her neck fretfully back and forth on the pillow. Then she patted the coverlet. "Sit down, Grace. I don't bite. I can't even raise myself. I'm just a house prisoner, lying flat on my back, like so many women through the ages. How tall are you, dear?"

"Mother—"

"I only noted she was *tall*, Katherine. Most models are freakishly tall—I was an exception." She closed her eyes a second. "Katherine's father has gone off to Durham for the day and left me to make the flower arrangements alone."

"Oh," I said.

"You mustn't apologize. I have simply outlived my own good taste. Haven't I, Katherine?"

Katherine gazed down at her bare feet, one crossed on top of the other.

"Outlived it, that's all—and sometimes I miss it."

I looked to Katherine for some help, but she was busy staring at her feet.

Mrs. Randolph's eyes shone in the dim

room like a cat's. "Some people are born without any taste, the way others are born homely, and they never even seem to notice. I envy them." She shut her eyes. "It's hot. I wish I knew why it's so hot. Do you know?"

I said I didn't.

"Well, don't judge us by our dog days. You aren't from Richmond, are you?" She picked at the bedspread and looked at me appraisingly. "I understand you're an artist. Do you paint?"

"She's a musician," Katherine said.

"Oh. Well, there'll be lots of nice loud music at Katherine's party. I'm sure you'll enjoy it. We'll have a long chat then. You remember, it's black tie or costume. I hope people aren't going to show up in tea-length. Of course with your height, it really doesn't matter. Are you sure you've never modeled?"

"No, ma'am."

"Well, you certainly have the height for it. And the personality. Katherine, shut the door gently when you leave, will you, baby? And fetch me a tall glass of ice. Just plain ice. With a twist of lemon. And fix your dress, honey. It's all bunched up and hanging on you like an ugly old drape. It was a pleasure meeting you, Grace." She lifted one hand and let it fall.

Katherine ushered me out of the room, shutting the door behind her. We wound our way farther into the house, along a bright hallway lined with windows and flowerpots filled with pink geraniums. Katherine's cotton dress made a hushed, slippery sound as she walked. She tugged at it halfheartedly, making some minuscule adjustment.

"You look fine," I said.

Katherine stopped walking. She leaned on the wall and pulled the chain of a hall lamp. The lamplight was lost in the glare from the windows.

"She hates me," she said.

A heavy silence fell between us. Katherine seemed gloomy; something of which I hadn't considered her capable. "She wants me to wear black to the coming-out party." She fiddled with the lamp chain. "Black crepe. She says it's sophisticated."

"Why not?" I said. "It's your funeral. Ha-ha."

Katherine managed a half-smile. "Do you want to see the party dresses?" she asked. "They're right upstairs."

"Sure, okay, I guess." I wanted to go home and take a nice cool shower, but I'd just gotten there. The Randolph house was even hotter and older than ours. I pushed my hair back from my face.

The bottled-up air of the upstairs hall rolled at us like a hammer blow. I followed Katherine into a tiny room, with a ceiling slanted so sharply I had to duck to get in. The furniture was white, painted with small sprays of flowers. It smelled like a mixture of talcum powder, cardboard, and a newly tarred road. It must have been 110 degrees in that little room.

Katherine smoothed a white cloth on the bed with her palm. When her hand passed over it, the cloth collapsed into the contours of a long white dress. Then I could see the others, all alike, long and lacy and white, laid across the white bedspread.

"I can't decide which one to keep," she said. The white dresses hung down to the floor, bodiless as tissue paper. Discreet white price tags dangled from the white dress straps. I looked from one to the other.

"Keep the black one," I said.

She lifted two of the white dresses and

held them up. They looked identical to me. Maybe one had a few more ruffles. I tried not to glance at the price tags.

"Let me show you the others." She laid the first two dresses down and picked up two more. They were all floor-length and ornate, like elongated snowflakes.

"What do you think?" she asked.

"They're all fine."

She held one up against her sundress and smoothed it out. "You like this one?" Her face rose above the white cloth, pale and unsmiling, like a face in a painting.

I'd always wondered what it would be like to be that beautiful—to be so lovely people would turn to stare at you or light up simply because you'd come into the room. It was too unlikely. I couldn't imagine it.

"What was it you wanted to ask me?" I said, more brusquely than I'd intended.

She lowered the dress, pushed the others aside, and sat on the bed. Her face relaxed for the first time since she'd met me at the door. "I need to ask a favor, Willie, about this party. It's going to sound stupid. —Actually, it's about Malachi. He's supposed to be my escort."

I let out an uneasy half-laugh because it sounded like she was going to ask something crazy—like what kind of corsage he should buy her—and because I suddenly felt frightened and I didn't know why.

"He can't be," she said.

"Did he change his mind?" I said.

"He doesn't even know about it yet."

"Oh." I stopped smiling. "So tell him."

"But what do I tell him?" she said, still clutching the dress and holding it out toward me as if I should take it.

"How should I know? I don't even know what you're talking about!" I felt so nervous that I jumped to my feet, looked around the room, and immediately sat down again. We were both half whispering, as if we thought someone might be hiding in the closet.

"He came up to visit a few weeks ago. It was a disaster. You've never seen anyone so out of place, Willie. My parents are still talking about it. I just can't embarrass them at this party, when everyone they know will be there. I'm not saying it's his fault—maybe it's his . . . background. I thought you could help me . . . being from the North and all."

The back of my neck prickled. I was listening and trying not to hear her at the same time. I jumped up again, walked to the window, keeping my back to her, and stared at the smooth green expanse of grass below. While I was standing there watching, the spray from an underground watering system shot up. The silvery arcs tossed themselves around in regularly rising and falling circles.

"You know how they are," she added. "I'll tell him your date couldn't make it. It's different for you, being from the North and all."

I turned to face her.

"Your parents wouldn't object to your spending one evening with—with a boy like Malachi."

I flinched, and hot as it was in that room, I felt chilled.

"I'm Jewish," I said. "I'm a Jew. Don't you know anything?"

Her face grew very still. Then at least she had the grace to blush.

"That's not what I meant, Willie," she said. "It was just—"

"I *know* what it was."

I could barely find the energy to lift one

sweaty arm, neatly swathed in blue oxford cloth, and attempt a perfunctory glance at my watch. "Look. I've got to go."

She stood up. "I'm so sorry. I only—"

"Shut up," I said. My arms were dangling down at my sides. I folded them across my chest. "Just show me how to get out of here."

She stood in her driveway watching while I backed the car out to the road. A squirrel darted across my path. I swerved, went up on her lawn, dragging tire marks across it. I tried to pretend none of it had happened; I wanted to go back and erase even the marks I had left on the grass.

Outside my own house, I stuffed the keys into my dress pocket and went straight into the air-conditioned kitchen. The cold air made me shiver. I drank down a glass of my mother's sugary lemonade-and-vodka concoction without stopping for breath, hoping it would make me instantly drunk. Nothing happened. I poured another. I could hear laughter—my mother had friends visiting. But no matter where I went or who I was with, I would always, always be alone.

"Did you have a nice time?" my mother called from the living room.

I pressed my hands against my forehead. "Yes!" I drained the rest of the drink, set the glass in the sink, and headed up the stairs.

"Willie?"

I pretended not to hear.

As soon as I got into my room, I stripped off my dress, balled it up in my hands, and kicked it into a corner. I turned on the radio and twisted the dial from station to station. Then I reached under my bed, groping among the dust mice, and fished out an old black saxophone case. I held it unopened on my chest, my fingertips resting lightly on the latch. Inside the case, on top of the sax, was a piece of dark blue velvet crumpled into a ball. It was a yarmulke that had belonged to my paternal grandfather, the musician—original owner of the Baldwin, the saxophone, the music. I smoothed out the skullcap and looked into it as if I were reading my own fortune. I laid it next to me on the bed.

On the last page of the telephone book, scribbled in pencil, was Malachi's phone number, something he'd left on a scrap of paper under my door a few days before I left school. As if by rote, I dialed the number.

He sounded far away and older, unlike

himself. "Steinberg!" he kept exclaiming in a deep voice. "Steinberg, what do you know! How are you?"

I came to the point right away.

"Spend the night?" he said. "Is this some kind of proposition? You're not even eighteen yet. Besides, you know, I'm here in Philadelphia."

"Not tonight, Malachi. The night of that coming-out party."

"Oh, that thing." He was quiet a minute. "I don't think I'm going. You know, Richmond's not my cup of tea. Did Katherine put you up to this?"

"No. So you shouldn't feel—"

"Wait," he said. "Let me think." I could practically hear him mulling it over. "I guess maybe I could come," he said.

"Don't if you don't want to," I said. "The truth is—"

"I want to," he said.

"It's awfully hot here," I said lamely.

"Look, Steinberg, you don't have to do this, you know. I'm not exactly a sparkling houseguest."

"Who cares?" I said. "I'm not a sparkling hostess. That's not the point."

"Isn't there a Holiday Inn there or something?"

"We have a big, empty house, Malachi. It's a lot like a Holiday Inn. Nobody will even know you're here."

He cleared his throat. "This is unexpectedly generous of you, Steinberg. —I mean, if you're sure. If it's absolutely no trouble to you or to any member of your family."

"I'll pick you up at the airport," I said.

"No, I'll take the train. I don't fly." He made a stab at sociability. "Did you get over what was wrong with you? You flunked some music class, didn't you?"

"Sort of."

"That's too bad. You all right now?"

"I'm fine," I said. "I'll see you in a few weeks, okay?"

"Sure, of course. This is your long-distance call. I could call you back—"

"No," I said. "—I mean, I was just on my way out."

"All right, then," he said. "This is very hospitable of you, Steinberg. Unexpected, really. I'll be in touch—I'll drop you a line."

We hung up. I collapsed back onto the bed. The saxophone case was still open at my side. I fitted the pieces together and tested my lip on the reed—and played a few old blues riffs I'd nearly forgotten. It's a strange fact about music that it changes your sense of time—you're pulled back into wherever you were when you last heard it. The saxophone made me feel about twelve years old, playing duets with my grandfather. Then I sat up, disassembled the instrument, stuffed the yarmulke inside, and latched the case shut again without even sliding it back under the bed. I pulled on a pair of shorts and one of my old painting shirts and went downstairs.

My mother was watering plants in the living room. Her friends had gone, leaving behind iced tea glasses and cookie crumbs. My mother was balanced precariously on a wooden stepladder. She'd tied up her hair in a red paisley scarf left over from her younger, wilder days. She turned around slowly to face me as I entered the room, cradling the watering can in both hands. Her face was pink from the heat and scrubbed looking as a girl's. There were times when I thought she looked younger than I did.

"Malachi Gelb is coming," I said in a voice of doom.

Undaunted, she poked a finger into the watering can and wiped the finger on her apron. "Oh? Fine. When?"

"The weekend of that debutante party. In late June. You remember."

"In June. I guess there'll be room."

"That's all we have in this house," I said. "Room."

She cocked her head at me and smiled coyly. "Well . . ."

"What?" I said.

"Well," she said again.

I stood looking up at her, dizzy. "Well, *what?*"

She stepped down off the ladder, swinging the watering can in one hand like a lantern. "Your father will be here," she said. "Remember?"

"Who?" I stared at her. "My *father*. What do you mean? When?"

She walked past me into the bathroom. "In late June. Didn't you read his card?"

I followed at her heels. "What card? You mean—a card? What are you talking about?"

A spider plant was sprawled in the middle of the bathroom sink. She began picking off the dead leaves and dumping them into the wastebasket. "His last postcard. What's the matter with you, Willie?"

I watched her hands moving among the leaves of the plant. "Nothing."

"You might at least sound happy." She went on with the plant, moved it a half-turn, and plucked some more leaves. She turned the faucet on. "He *is* your father, you know."

"I'm surprised," I said. "That's all."

Her forehead wrinkled. There was a faint, high humming sound in my ears, the water running.

"I worry about you sometimes," she said. I had to read her lips saying it. She shut off the faucet, lifted the plant, and walked back to the living room, holding it up in front of her.

I trailed behind, staring over the top of her head, the bright-colored scarf. It was so important to stay calm. My eyes came to rest on an antique clock on the living room mantel. I watched the round brass pendulum swing steadily back and forth, with its muffled *dock-dock dock-dock*. I stared around the room like someone looking for an emergency exit in a fire. "I guess I'd better practice," I finally said.

"We'll have to think about emptying that study soon!" she called after me.

I pulled the study door shut behind me and threw the bolt. Everything was in its place. The kids played next door in bright summer clothing, their voices shrill as crickets. I swung one arm across the piano lid, sweeping everything onto the hardwood floor. Mozart landed sideways with a crash. Papers scattered at my feet. The fall had set the cello strings vibrating in their corner of the room, humming inside the closed case. Something else was making a ticking sound. I looked down. The rosewood metronome had split neatly along one glued seam, so I could see the delicate, spiderlike inner workings of the machinery; but it had landed upright and was still counting out the seconds—it hadn't skipped a beat.

Chapter Four

MALACHI'S TRAIN was forty minutes late coming into the Richmond station. I was standing at the snack bar, nursing a lukewarm Coke when he arrived, and didn't see him till he was halfway across the waiting room. He looked different, worried, taller and even thinner, more like a grown man. He was dragging a huge yellow suitcase and a silver garment bag. When I called his name, he jerked around as if someone had poked him in the back.

"*Steinberg!*" he cried. His voice bounced off the high marble walls. "Why didn't you warn me about the heat?" People turned to look.

The temperature had edged above 100 degrees that morning. Malachi wore a tweed jacket over a yellow sport shirt—his green wool scarf protruded from the pocket like a hanky—and his mouth and eyes were rimmed with sweat. The blue cap with the Communist China star on the brim sat back on his head. His long black shoes gleamed as if he'd gotten a shoe shine right there on the train.

I walked over to him, and we shook hands solemnly and a little awkwardly. "Welcome to sunny Richmond," I said.

"How do they expect people to survive in this heat? Do you know they don't even air-condition the trains? An old woman fainted on her way to Miami. You look a little better than you did, by the way."

I lifted his suitcase. My arm dropped down to the floor. "What's in here?" I asked. "Lead weights?"

"Just a few books," he said uneasily. "A few gifts. Steinberg, put it down, please. You can carry this." He gestured with the garment bag. "This has just my suit; it's lighter."

I hung on to the suitcase "No, this is okay."

Malachi lowered the garment bag to the

floor. It flopped over on one side, like some-body fainting. "Steinberg, I insist! Carry the suit!"

People were beginning to stare. I ex-changed bags with him. "The car's right out-side," I said. "It's air-conditioned."

"Thank God!" Malachi glanced around the high-domed station, shaking his head, making loud *tsk*ing sounds. "This must be Robert E. Lee's mausoleum, right? Where is he buried? Under the tracks?"

I noticed a narrow white box that stuck out of his jacket pocket. He saw me looking at it.

"Oh, this," he said, touching it with one hand. "It's not for you. Sorry."

"I didn't think it was."

"Here, wait," he said. "I want you to see it." He lowered his suitcase to the marble floor. It was bound with rope and rocked like a boat when he set it down. A wave of hot air shuddered past us as the station doors swung opened and closed. He tapped the long white box. "It's for Katherine. A black orchid," he said. His sly, troutlike smile stretched the corners of his mouth.

"You're kidding."

"I'm not. They're extremely rare." He mopped his face with the end of the green wool scarf. He extracted the box from his pocket. Very gently, he worked open the lid. Inside lay something that looked like a crumpled, filthy tissue.

"I can see why," I said.

Malachi stared at it in horror. "It's dead."

"What?"

"Look at it! It's completely dead!"

I put one hand out. "Let me see." I touched the orchid lightly with my fingertip, and one edge crumbled away. "Why didn't you pack it in ice or something?"

Malachi stared at it blankly. "I bought it at a florist's right next to the Philadelphia train station. The man in the store said it would bloom for days." He shook his head. "Dead! I can't believe it."

"So buy her another one."

"I can't. Where?" He touched the flower and another piece crumbled loose. "They're very rare, the man said, and this one cost me thirty dollars."

"Then get her daisies or something."

"It's not the same."

"So give it to her that way."

He replaced the lid, and stuck the box back in his jacket pocket. "That orchid was still flourishing when we passed through Baltimore, Maryland," he said. "It's an omen."

"Come on, Malachi. You don't believe in omens."

He smiled bleakly. "Only in the bad ones," he said.

Malachi and my mother greeted each other like long-lost friends and companions. He drew out a pair of silver candlesticks and a box of scented soaps from his suitcase and presented them to her as house gifts. They had met a few times up at school—he'd joined us for dinner one night, at the school cafeteria—and now they resumed their acquaintance like veterans of the same foreign war. When I walked into a room, I was greeted by abrupt silences and glassy looks or, worse yet, vivacious smiles, and finally realized this meant they'd been talking about me; I was their common cause. After I left, there'd be one or two whispered exchanges, then the volume would return to normal.

I had never watched Malachi try to charm anyone, and if the effect hadn't been so grotesque, it might have been impressive. He entertained my mother with long, fictional anecdotes about the Randolph family and kept her glass refilled with lemonade and vodka; when the temperature rose to new heights that afternoon, he even offered to run to the store for more ice.

"Let him run," I said. "It'd be good for him."

They both looked up and through me, and went back to their conversation.

"You know, in certain parts of rural Virginia, slavery didn't actually end till the late 1950s," Malachi was telling my mother.

I kept wandering back upstairs to study the party dress laid out on my bed, hoping that long, steady scrutiny would improve it, or at least make it passable. It was a floor-length sleeveless *gown*—there was no other word for it—with a matching flowered jacket. The only good thing about the dress was that it had pockets. My mother had picked it out for me while I stood on top of a pedestal in a boutique dressing room, surrounded by petite salesgirls, like Gulliver among the Lilliputians. It was possible for me to walk if I took shuffling little steps and didn't ever lift my feet. The jacket exactly matched the dress, but the sleeves were at least an inch too short.

"*Look* at this," I told my mother when we got the thing home. "You can see my wrists!"

"Only if you keep sticking them out."

"This dress is *brown*. Whoever heard of a brown formal? I look like a freak."

"You look lovely."

"I look like a telephone pole with flowers climbing all over it."

Whenever I was feeling miserable, I went up to my room to look at the outfit, and every time I looked at it, I felt more miserable.

I was trying to steel myself, too, for the likelihood of my father not showing up again— or of suddenly showing up. He could do that. He was unpredictable. On Father's Day at music camp one year he arrived a day early, wearing shorts and Italian sunglasses. I was so embarrassed by the sight of his pale, hairy legs, his efforts to charm the camp director and everyone else, that I went and hid in the woods. At my first cello recital he came so late he missed everything but the last smattering of applause.

I felt a hand on my shoulder and jumped. It was Malachi.

"Here," he said, and handed me a weather-beaten paperback.

"What is this?"

"It's a book. You've seen one before, probably."

I read the title. *Women in Music.* "No thanks," I said. "I'm interested in music. Not women in music. *Music.* Period."

"You can't pretend issues like gender and religion don't exist, Steinberg." He peered over my shoulder into the room. "Pretty dress. Is it yours?"

"Yes," I said curtly.

"I'm surprised you're not wearing armor."

"I'm surprised you're going at all," I said.

He glanced at me quizzically. "Your mother said something about cleaning out a room today. You need help?"

"No!" I said. "Just leave me alone, okay?"

He lifted both hands, palms out. "Touchy!" He headed back downstairs.

I sat on the edge of my bed holding the paperback. It was marked up all over with marginalia. He'd even scrawled my name, "Steinberg!" a few times, with arrows pointing at the text. It gave me a strange sensation, to see my name in his handwriting. I read one of the marked passages: ". . . they must struggle in the face of a prejudice against their possession of genius so deep-rooted and widespread that even their faith in themselves wavers, and the desire to attain without which no goal can be made is thus shorn of the strong impulse that should 'aim at the stars' and is content if it but 'hits the moon.' " I shut the book and sat staring at my dress and jacket.

While Malachi and my mother were busy talking in the kitchen, I snuck into the music room. I stood in the center of the room, studying its peacefulness, its order. I stood very still, taking it all in for future use. I felt as if I'd betrayed the place by not using it properly—a sensation I'd had in the practice rooms at school—and there was a yearning, suddenly, to make it all right. Even the glued-together Mozart bust seemed to be urging something on me. I stood racking my brains, staring into the corners as if the answer might be present in the room. But time was running out again.

I climbed the stairs to the attic, dusted off my father's portfolios, his sample cases, ledgers, and maps, and carried it all back downstairs by the armload. I dragged my own things into my room and shoved them under the bed, where I wouldn't have to look at them yet. The cello I leaned in a corner of the room, near the closet. It hummed eerily inside its case from having been moved.

As one of Katherine's two official escorts, Malachi was due at the party an hour before anyone else. By five o'clock he was pacing up and down in the kitchen, sipping his glass of lemonade, swallowing hard, as if it were made of ground glass, sipping again. His conversation faltered and finally dragged to a halt altogether. He excused himself and went up to his room—to catch up on some reading, he croaked, his voice barely audible. He looked bad, even for him. I knocked on his door a few minutes later. He didn't answer. "Are you okay?" I asked. I thought I heard a faint reply.

I cracked the door open. Malachi was stretched out on top of the bed, asleep, the navy blue cap pulled down over his eyes. It was startling to see him lying so still. He slept heavily, with his mouth half open and his bony hands folded across his chest like a corpse, his shiny black shoes bending his ankles off the edge of the bed.

I wandered around the hot upstairs hall, moving nervously from one room to another, lighting up cigarettes and stubbing them out again, untouched, leaving a trail of tobacco smoke. My mother followed close at my heels, cleaning the ashtrays. She'd washed her hair and let it down loose that morning, and she had a bright, eager look in her eyes. I avoided talking about my father or the party, though I could tell she wanted to talk about both, and finally, to forestall conversation altogether, I ducked into the bathroom for my third long lukewarm shower of the day.

When I got downstairs, my mother was sitting by herself at the kitchen table, hands folded on the tabletop. A copy of the Modern Library edition of *Out of Africa* lay open in front of her, the pages riffling a little in the breeze from the air conditioner. She looked up as soon as I walked in, as if she'd been waiting in ambush for me.

"Feel better?" she asked. "Nice and cool?"

"Yes, fine." I swung open the refrigerator, looked in, nodded politely to everything inside, and closed it. At school I ran track and played tennis, I thought, and in Richmond I lay around in the heat and ate.

"There's some nice fresh cake," she offered.

"I'm not hungry," I said—too sharply, from the wounded look on her face.

"Willie." She decided to come to the point. "Try to act friendly when your father gets home."

"Friendly?" I sat opposite her at the kitchen table, my hands flat on the table.

My mother was sitting exactly the same way, across from me.

"You deal," I said.

Her eyes grew large and light. The lines at the corners deepened.

"Listen," I said at last, sighing. "Do we have to discuss this? It's not worth it. He'll call at the last minute and say something came up. How many times has he done that already?"

"I don't know. I haven't counted."

"Well, I have. Take my word for it." She said nothing. Her lack of response maddened me. "For God's sakes! Don't you have any pride? Why do you sit around here waiting for him? You're young, you're still attractive, you're not stuck. There must be *something* else you can do."

"Stop, Willie." She waved one hand at me, then groped the hand across the tabletop for a Kleenex. The box was a few feet away, on the counter. I went and got it for her.

"I'm sorry," I said. I was, too. I stooped awkwardly beside her, one hand propped on the back of her chair to steady myself.

She blew her nose, then folded the tissue into quarters. "I forget how young you are," she said. "You were fourteen when we moved here. You don't really even know your father."

"I don't want to know him, either."

"Oh, Willie." She shook her head. "You're so much alike."

"I'm not like him," I said. "He's a son of a bitch."

That startled us both into silence, for a second.

"No, he isn't," she said slowly. "And I know what you're thinking, but you've seen too many movies." She shook her head. "Women are not your father's vice."

I waited, my throat tight. The room seemed very quiet. "So what is?"

She looked past me, out through the kitchen door as if someone were standing there. I turned to look. The yard was white with late-afternoon sunlight. "Ambition, Willie. Same as yours. Overwhelming ambition."

She pushed back her chair, scraping it on the linoleum, and stood up, so I stood, too. She looked small, as she always did when we stood side by side. "And don't worry about being what you are," she added.

"What's that?"

She surprised me by smiling. "His daughter," she said.

She held my face for a minute, then kissed my cheek. I towered over her, looking down into the pale roots of her hair. Her face was young-looking and unmarked, as if she'd never had a sulky child or a failed marriage, any of it.

After I'd heard her footsteps fade over my head, I rummaged around downstairs looking for my father's last postcard. It was still where I'd last seen it, on the hall table. The giant hotel on the front turned out to be the downtown Chicago Marriott. I hid the card in the palm of my hand, magician style, and carried it up to my room and closed and locked the door behind me. I didn't know what I would say if I got him on the phone; I couldn't think that far ahead.

I dialed slowly, keeping my finger in the dial hole and wincing at the noise of the clicks. The Richmond operator and then Illinois Information kept begging me to speak up, but I couldn't raise my voice above a hoarse whisper.

By the time I'd scribbled the Hilton phone number on a piece of trash paper, my hands were shaking so hard I had to settle the phone back in the cradle and just sit a minute. I was afraid my father had never been in Chicago. Sometimes it seemed to me he wasn't even real anymore—that we had made him up. Maybe he was dead, and all the calls we got were old recorded messages.

"I'm sorry," the Hilton receptionist told me, "but you'll have to speak up."

"I'm calling for Mr. Paul Steinberg—he's with the Apsquith Pharmaceutical Corporation. I'm his daughter," I whispered hoarsely.

"Moment, please." The phone clicked dead, and Muzak chimed through the receiver. I held the phone away from my ear and thumbed through the *Women in Music* book lying beside me on the bed, my eyes jumping from one marked passage to the next. I read from Clara Schumann's diary: "Of course, it is only a woman's work, which is always lacking in force, and here and there in invention." I turned back a page. "I once thought that I possessed creative talent, but I have given up on this idea; a woman must not desire to compose—not one has been able to do it, and why should I expect to? It would be arrogance indeed, though my father led me into it in earlier days."

I threw the book down on the bed.

Both my bedroom windows faced west, so the hot sunlight fell directly on my face. My mind was racing but nothing came clear. The tinny mosquito whine of the Muzak violins switched to the plinking of a piano. Halfway into that, the phone clicked and the hotel operator came back on. "Miss?"

My stomach rose up and flopped over.

It felt like a long time before she spoke. "Your father checked out this morning."

"Did he by any chance say where he was going? I'm his daughter. —It's important."

"I just came on," the woman said. "Is this a family emergency? I can check with a morning clerk."

"Yes, it is. Thank you. —Wait!" I said, but she'd already switched the Muzak back on. I hid the receiver under the bedcovers. After a long wait I heard a tiny human voice chirping from the bed.

I snatched up the phone. "Yes?"

"Your father checked out at eleven. He gave a home address in Richmond, Virginia. I'm afraid that's all the information we have."

"Okay," I said. "Thanks." My breathing changed. I felt happy, hopeful. For the first time in two years I remembered what my father's face looked like.

I was conscious of the late, hot sunlight falling on my forearm. Down the street came the faraway *ting* of an ice-cream truck. With it, a wash of remembered childhood summer afternoons came flooding back, along with that unreal bright sense of anticipatory joy, vaguely associated with daylong softball games and evening piano lessons. I remembered a lightweight black jacket with gold buttons my mother dressed me in every spring when the weather got warm enough. For a second or two

I lost track of who and where I was. Then I heard the hotel operator breathing in my ear.

"What's it like in Chicago?" I asked her. "Is it nice and cool?"

The dial tone hummed in my ears. I replaced the phone in its cradle and looked at the hotel number. I turned the piece of scrap paper over and smoothed it out. On the back was a half-page of music. I recognized my own handwriting, but that was all. I couldn't even remember writing it down. I got off the bed and rummaged around in the trash looking for more, but that was it—just a few measures scribbled in pencil. When I held a pen in my hand and looked at it again, the music seemed to slide somewhere else, as if into the darkness under a waterfall. I dropped the paper onto my bed, scared. I could feel the rest of the music, waiting, pulled tight in the cords of my hands and feet.

My mother was moving around downstairs in the kitchen, opening and closing cupboards and drawers. I lifted my typewriter up, slid the paper underneath, and settled the machine on top. The music felt safer there, hidden, weighted down.

I lay down on my bed, pushing the jacket

and dress aside, and the next thing I knew my mother was knocking on the bedroom door, calling my name.

I woke with my head resting on the shoulder of the flowered jacket like an old friend. The music was still in my head, as if I'd been dreaming about it. I checked under the typewriter first thing. The paper was wrinkled but pressed flat, the dark notes scattered like bullets across the page.

Remembering the call to my father's hotel came a few seconds later, and felt less real. When I pulled the door of my room closed, it seemed as if I had left the phone call behind me like a movie. Then there was nothing ahead but the party looming up, a brick wall.

My mother and I waited for Malachi at the bottom of the stairs. He paced behind the guest-room door, the closet door rolling open and shut, calling to us every few seconds, "I'll be out, I'll be right out!" Finally the door of the guest room opened and he came down.

"Mr. America," he announced, stepping gingerly off the bottom stair.

His bright red hair was brushed down flat. It curled up behind his ears like something making fun of him behind his back. The big double-breasted black suit he wore hung loose; the sleeves reached almost to his second knuckle. A sad-looking black bow tie dangled at his throat like an old man's. I'd never seen him without the red-starred cap on his head, and his naked skull looked elongated and fragile.

He shrugged at our expression. "There wasn't time to go to a tailor," he said. His tone was a mixture of arrogance and terror. "Do I look all right?" He turned around. The back of his coat, split over his thin rear end, was shiny with age and covered with dog hairs. The whole outfit looked like something he'd dug up from a grave. My mother drew in her breath.

"You look fine!" she said quickly. "Wonderful!"

He turned to face us again, his eyes narrowed. "I look okay? Steinberg—you think?"

I nodded. "Swell."

"Just let me get a clothes brush to touch you up," my mother murmured. "Don't go anywhere. Wait here!" She hurried off.

Malachi and I were left standing in silence looking at each other. The odor of

mothballs emanating from his suit was overwhelming.

"Nice," I said. "Very nice."

"I've looked in a mirror," Malachi said.
"It's nothing to write home about." He
reached into his jacket pocket and drew out
a white oblong box. "Steinberg, I want to show
you something. Look."

He lifted the top of the box, and the orchid—or what was left of it—lay inside the
tissue paper, dissolved into a heap of black
dust.

"You showed me," I said. "She'll have a
hard time pinning it to her dress, though."

"Wrong. Wrong box," he said testily. He
tucked it back into his pocket, slapped himself on the chest a few times, then drew a
smaller satin jeweler's case from his breast
pocket, holding it out to me. "Quick! Before
your mother gets back! Open it."

I looked at the shiny box. *"You* open it,"
I said.

He adjusted the black elastic of his bow
tie. "Go ahead. It's a surprise."

I took the case reluctantly.

He smiled. "Open it!"

I pushed open the lid with both thumbs. Inside, on a pale pink satin cushion, lay a gold ring with a tiny diamond chip in it: an engagement ring. For one paralyzing split second I thought it was a present for me. I felt a disconcerting mixture of appalled emotions. I almost asked out loud, "For me?"—and then I realized of course it was for Katherine. My whole body grew faint and hot with embarrassment at what I'd nearly done. My face flushed. I slapped the box shut.

"There's something I should tell you," I said.

"Don't look so grim," he said.

"It's about Katherine."

His expression sharpened, but he kept looking at me, steadily. "She's engaged," he said.

"I don't think so."

"She's pregnant. She's dying."

"No, no," I said. "Nothing like that."

"Okay, then. I don't need to hear it." He took the pink box from my hands, closed it, and tucked it back into his breast pocket.

"I just hope you didn't buy that ring from the guy who sold you the orchid," I said.

He gazed somewhere over my shoulder. A muscle in his jaw twitched.

"Were you going to give that to her to-night?"

He nodded. I could see the ends of his fingertips thrusting from the black sleeves of his coat, and they were visibly vibrating, bumping against one another. I could picture how thrilled she'd be to get that ring in front of everyone—she and her whole family.

"Malachi, look," I said. "This is a big night for her. It's going to be hectic. Why don't you hold off?"

He squinted at me. "What are you—jeal-ous?" I decided not to dignify that with a reply.

"Timing is everything," he said. "This is her debut. This is where I make my move."

"Just wait a while. A little time never hurt anything."

"Ha!" He leaned forward and gripped the banister. He stared at his hand resting on the polished wood, the black sleeve hanging down eerily like crepe over the oak knob. "A little time is what *kills* people," he said. "Don't you know that?"

"That's one way of looking at it," I said.

He narrowed his eyes at me over the banister as if he was about to launch another harangue on my faults. Instead he said, "Suppose Einstein was wrong. Suppose time is a movable element—like water or air. Then history would be fluid, right? All human suffering, all events happening at the same time. We could pour one hour to the next without spilling a drop. Nothing would ever be lost. No one. We could raise the dead—just reach out in time and haul them back." He snatched at the air, then rubbed his hand back and forth through his hair. His face, which had brightened as he spoke, grew sullen and ugly. "Except that's impossible. You can't wash twice from the same faucet, Heracleitus says. And even if you could, it wouldn't be the same hand. Even if time's only a human construct—we're only human. We're stuck, Steinberg. Time isn't fluid; it's a poisoned cup. I've got to ask her tonight."

"Wait a week. A week is nothing."

"In a week I'll lose my nerve," he said. "Or my appetite. Carpe diem! Seize the girl."

"Good things come to those who wait," I said.

I heard my mother's footsteps approach, then hesitate, then come forward again.

"Malachi, turn around," she said, looking at me strangely when he did. "I'll have you all fixed up in a second."

"No, no." He pushed back his coat sleeve and consulted a large yellow-faced watch. "No. Thank you, but I have to go."

"Just stand still." My mother gripped his shoulder, rotated him a quarter-turn, and brushed with the other. She stepped back and adjusted the rear flap of his jacket. "It could use a little pressing," she said, as if someone had forced the admission from her.

Malachi struggled loose. He was so nervous he was panting like a runner. "Mrs. Steinberg, thank you, but I've got to go. I promised I'd be there by seven. Seven o'clock."

"This'll only take a second," she said.

"Too late," I said. "Between seven and seven-oh-one our hostess could be poisoned."

My mother gave me a warning look. "All right, Malachi. Have a good time. You've got the keys?"

He held them up. The keys shook in his hand.

"I'm not sure Mr. Steinberg's Buick is still insured, so don't get into any accidents." She laughed nervously. "Don't get into any accidents anyway."

"There are no accidents," I told her. "We're all doomed. Stuck."

"You'll be fine," my mother told Malachi. "Just take it easy. Please. Both of you. Relax."

"Right." Malachi avoided my eyes and touched his breast pocket. "I'll see you at the party, Steinberg. Save me the last waltz."

My mother walked him out to the porch. It was barely dusk, but the sky was turning a deep silken blue.

Malachi and my mother murmured together on the front lawn for a few seconds; then she came back through the door into the foyer and stood next to me, her hand lightly on my arm. We waited for his footsteps on the gravel and then the sound of the old Buick's engine turning over, pulling away. My mother tightened her hand around my elbow. "Oh dear God," she sighed. "That poor, unfortunate boy."

Chapter Five

MY ESCORT FOR the evening was a distant cousin of Katherine's. His name was Arthur, but when he called to confirm our date, he asked me to please call him Walrus. He was engaged to be married in August, but for reasons too complex and Southern for me to follow, his own fiancée was going to the party with *her* cousin. By eight o'clock he still hadn't arrived. I was wearing makeup and perfume, and bore only a faint resemblance to my normal self. I kept expecting my father would walk in and think I had gotten dressed up this way for him. It was all I could do to keep from running outside and waiting for Walrus on the street corner.

My mother set up a game of Scrabble to pass the time. I kept my face aimed at the front door, jerking back at the sound of every passing car. There was an odor of lemon furniture polish in the room so powerful, it seemed to be masking something we had buried under the rug. I felt a periodic stabbing in my chest—what I half feared and half hoped must be a heart attack—and the insides of my mouth kept drawing in, as if I were sucking on the lemon polish. My mother saw all my twitches and grimaces and let me win the first game of Scrabble, then threw the second one, too. I was listening so hard for outside noises that she had to poke me, both times, just to remind me the game was over.

Still, when the doorbell rang it came like a gunshot. I jumped up as if I'd been hit. My mother walked slowly to the door, while I stuffed the Scrabble set into the china cupboard and raced into the kitchen.

A low Southern voice I didn't recognize said good evening to my mother and murmured his way into the living room. I stood in the kitchen for a second, wobbling on my high heels, then put on my jacket and walked back out. The pale young man standing next to my mother wore a white tuxedo and a red cummerbund around his thin waist. He resembled one of those porcelain dolls you see on top of wedding cakes. He bowed directly from the cummerbund as I entered. He had sparse, fine hair, almost white, balding back from his forehead, and large white front teeth. I was at least three inches taller than he was.

"You must be Grace!" he said, showing the teeth. He ducked, nodding his head, as if to avoid a blow. "Walrus. I'm so very sorry I'm late. I've just been apologizing to your mother." He spoke softly, with that curious Richmond accent halfway between British and a Southern drawl, putting out one long white hand to me. "I understand you people are not from Richmond originally."

"We're from Connecticut," my mother said. She looked at me defiantly, as if I might deny it.

"Well, this is a pleasure," Walrus said, finally letting go of my hand. "We don't often have an opportunity to meet our friends from up North. I've surely been looking forward to tonight, let me tell you. May I present you with this?" He handed me a corsage, still cool and dewy from the inside of a refrigerator.

"Thank you," I said. Somewhere along the line I'd forgotten to say hello, or how are you, and it seemed too late to work it in.

Walrus hummed under his breath, off tune, as he struggled to pin the corsage to my dress. I think it was a hymn. Every time we moved, we bumped together in some intimate way. His upper lip began to sweat. Finally I took the flowers back out of his hands and pinned them to the shoulder of my jacket.

"They're gardenias. I hope you like them." Walrus put his hands in his pockets.

"They're very nice," I said. "Flowers. Thanks."

An awkward silence developed.

"The Randolphs have a sixth sense for arranging a social occasion—they always have had," Walrus said. "It's a beautiful evening for a dance, don't you think?"

"Beautiful," my mother said.

The three of us made an awkward huddle in the living room. Eventually I edged toward the front door. Walrus opened it and flattened himself against the screen door, gesturing for me to walk on ahead.

"Don't stay out too late," my mother said. "You know, with your father—" She broke off at the expression on my face. "You just never know," she finished lamely.

"Isn't that the truth?" Walrus said. "But don't worry, ma'am, I'll have Grace back sober and safe at a proper hour." (He pronounced it as "proppah.") "You go on and enjoy your own evening. It's been a pleasure meeting you."

"You, too," my mother said. She had on her shiniest company smile. She aimed it at me. "Have a nice time, Willie."

"Oh, I'm sure I will," I said. Walrus was still standing flat against the screen door with his arm stuck out straight. I went ahead of him.

The sky had darkened to violet blue, with bars of red at the horizon. The tree frogs were tuning up for the night.

Walrus stood so close to me he was practically stepping on the heels of my shoes.

"May I carry your jacket?" he said.

"No thanks," I said. "I'm still wearing it."

He guffawed as if I'd made a joke, and took my arm. We stopped in front of a long white Thunderbird, its two right-hand tires perched on the curb. "Here we are," he said. He opened the door on my side. When I sat, the sleeves of my jacket hitched up an extra two inches. I stared down at my wrists, then at the tips of my shoes, a thousand miles away.

"Let me know if it gets too drafty for you here." Walrus stuck his head out the window to check for traffic. There was a little U. Va. banner where the side mirror should have been.

We bumped gently down off the curb and eased onto the street, instantly picking up speed. My hair blew straight back from my face. Walrus took Monument Avenue at sixty-five.

"You know the story behind these old statues?" he asked me. The statues whipped past. Walrus referred to the Civil War as "the War Between the States" and made it sound like something that had happened a few weeks earlier. He spoke in a series of breathless exclamations. I twisted around to watch General Stuart flying by.

"Jeb Stuart! He was a crazy young upstart. Oh, he was the darling of Lee!" We veered up onto the interstate, cutting off another car. The driver blasted his horn. Walrus lifted an arm and waved. He draped the arm on the seat behind me, almost but not quite touching my shoulder. He held the steering wheel delicately between the thumb and forefinger of his left hand.

"Grace," he said. "As we are driving along, I want to show you a few of the local sights. You'll like this. We'll be passing by the house of Mr. Edgar Poe pretty soon. You're a poet, aren't you?"

"Musician," I said.

" 'I was a child and she was a child, in this kingdom by the sea—' There!" He lifted his hand off the wheel and pointed. "That house right there!" The car bounced along the soft shoulder of the highway. I watched a row of brick houses career by. "Did you get a good look at it?" he asked.

"Yes," I lied. My spine was pressed flat against the seat.

"And that pretty little one is where his mistress used to live—if you'll pardon my saying so. Liked to keep her close by, I guess." He snuck a look at me.

"What's your fiancée's name?" I asked.

"Maryanne. Sweet Maryanne."

We rode along in silence for a minute. The wind beat at my face like an enormous powder puff. At one point I clocked the car at seventy-five.

"You know, Grace, there's a sizable Jewish population here in Richmond. Very old, very proper families. They've done fine things for the city—some of those fellows are fixing up the houses down by the water. Smart investments. After the party, I'd be glad to show you. Give you a proper tour."

We pulled into a parking lot as big as the lot for the Connecticut State Fair. It was already half filled with long, pastel-colored American sedans. Walrus shut off the engine and sat there a minute with one arm over the back of my seat. The car engine ticked softly, cooling down, like a clock. The windows of the car were wide open and the hot smell of tar rose up around us, making it hard to catch my breath.

Walrus touched my arm. "Relax," he said. "It's just a party. I won't let them cook you up and eat you."

The outside of the Arena looked like some enormous airplane hangar. Inside, it more closely resembled an overgrown school gymnasium. Its entrance was a maze of bright lights and guests, the air inside so hot and thick it felt like a fifth element against my skin. Walrus and I were forcibly separated by the jostling crowd. Katherine and her family stood near the door receiving the guests. A flashbulb lit Katherine's face every few seconds, as if she were standing in the middle of a summer lightning storm. She wore a black dress with spaghetti straps that kept falling down onto her arms. Mrs. Randolph was in something sequined and orange and knee-length. An unhappy-looking little girl wearing white gloves stood half hidden just behind her. A man I took to be Mr. Randolph stood at attention by the little girl's side.

I spotted Malachi off to one side of the room, jammed against the wall, perhaps six feet away, surrounded by guests. Every now and then he'd rise up on his tiptoes to try and see over the heads of the crowd. No one in the Randolph family glanced his way except once—when the photographer called for a group photo, he tried to push forward, and Mr. Randolph waved him away. At that point he disappeared from view. I tried to see where he'd gone, but we were packed in so tightly I could barely move. I could not remember how I'd ever been talked into this.

Someone laid a hand on my wrist. "Gotcha!" Walrus said. His bone-pale forehead was already damp with sweat. He helped me off with my jacket and folded it over one thin arm. "I had to find Maryanne. She's dying to meet you. Did you see Sid Randolph's flapper outfit? She must be melting under all those sequins!"

As he spoke he guided me swiftly through the crowd. Katherine kissed Walrus and squeezed my hand hard in her white-gloved one.

"I'm so glad you all could come," she said. She clung to my hand like a shipwreck survivor, and we both flinched as the photographer's bulb went off in our faces. I blinked at a young man who had materialized at Katherine's side like a genie out of a bottle. His forehead was wrapped in a huge white bandage. He had a face like Walrus's, but smaller and younger, more perfectly handsome. He reached out to shake my hand just as Walrus walked me a few steps forward, so I ended up half bowing instead in front of Mrs. Randolph. She stared at me blankly, without recognition. "We're so thrilled you could come!" she cried. She pushed the little girl forward. "This is

Katherine's baby sister, Bly. She'll be coming out next."

Bly and I stood studying each other. She tentatively put out one big, white-gloved hand, like a paw. I shook it. Her feet were enormous, puppyish, in clumsy white bow-tie pumps. Someday she was going to be six feet tall, easy. She seemed to think so, too, by the way she was sizing me up. "How do you do?" she said. "Are you from Richmond?"

"Not originally."

Mr. Randolph stuck out his hand and shook mine, staring at the front of my dress.

"From up North, aren't you?" he said. "How'd you come down?"

"I live here in Richmond," I said.

He studied me, concentrating on the middle of my forehead this time. "That's not possible," he said flatly. He turned to his younger daughter. "Is she from New York? Sounds like New York City to me."

Bly acted as if she hadn't heard. "Would you like to watch TV with me?" she asked. "There's a good program on."

"Not now." Walrus returned to reclaim my arm. "You all had better let me introduce my

date to my fiancée, before I get strung up."
He laughed, showing his front teeth.

Bly stood on her tiptoes to call after me.
"It was very nice meeting you!"

"You see?" Walrus said. "You've already
made a conquest. Now don't run off. I'll go
fetch Maryanne." He gave my arm a squeeze
and headed off into the crowd at a slow trot,
carrying my flowered jacket over his arm.

The dance floor was a tiny circle in the
middle of the Arena, marked off by masking
tape and colored lights. One elderly couple
fox-trotted around inside it, heads down, as if
they were looking for something they had
dropped. A five-piece band was playing old
songs slightly off tempo. At the moment they
were slogging through "The Yellow Rose of
Texas."

I caught a glimpse of Malachi, next to the
bar by this time, leaning in a corner behind
a beer keg. His red hair bobbed in and out
of sight among the milling guests. They held
their drinks up in the air like Olympic
torches. I pushed my way over to him.

We shook hands for the second time that
day. He smelled powerfully of scotch and

sweat. "Loveliness, thy name is Steinberg," he intoned.

"You're drunk."

He lifted his plastic glass. "Two lousy scotches. These anti-Semites won't serve me."

"You might try standing on line," I said.

He smiled unpleasantly. "I've been waiting for you to show up, Steinberg. Go ahead and get me another scotch. You have that Aryan look; you can pass."

While the bartender fixed the scotch, I drank a glass of champagne and then another. There were bowls of iced shrimp lined along the bar, so I brought back a napkinful of those, balanced on top of the two glasses.

Malachi gazed moodily into the napkin. "Shellfish," he said. "That stuff's *treyf.* Don't you know anything, Steinberg?"

"There's plenty of peanuts if you want some." We stood elbow to elbow and gazed out at the crowd.

"Even the peanuts here are *treyf.* Not a Jew in the crowd."

"They'll be holding evening services later," I said. "Just for the two of us."

"If they did, you wouldn't show. You'd be at church, listening to the organ music."

Old women in watered-silk dresses shuffled around the outskirts of the Arena fanning themselves with cocktail napkins.

"Walking heart attacks," Malachi said, smiling grimly. "My grandmother died of heart failure."

"So did mine," I said.

Malachi swirled his drink and smirked. "Grandparents, Steinberg! I thought you sprang full grown from Beethoven's frown."

Walrus walked by, his arm through the arm of a tall, willowy girl with short blond hair. She looked remarkably like him, except that she was dressed like a tropical bird, in lime green, gold, orange, and white.

"That's my date," I said.

Malachi gazed over the rim of his glass. "Which one?"

"He's Katherine's cousin."

"Looks like the product of too much inbreeding." Malachi glanced at Walrus again, frowned, then looked away. He poked at the ice in his drink with a forefinger. "Blood is thicker than ice."

"Warmer, too," I said.

"Speaking of blood," he said. "Your mother's a charming woman. Now I'm most anxious

to meet your father. As Nietzsche once said,
'What was silent in the father speaks in the
child and often I have found the child the
unveiled secret of the father.' And vice versa,
of course."

"How's Katherine doing?" I asked.

"Oh, great," he said. A pained expression
flickered across his face; then he smiled.
"She waved at me, I think. One time. She and
the sheik of Araby."

"Who?"

"The sheik, the sheik," he said impatiently. The *sh* made a whistling sound. "He
comes from a long line of stockbrokers. Two
escorts. The Arab and the Jew. They've got a
peculiar sense of humor down here. He's
wearing a sheet around his head—left over
from the last cross-burning party, I'll bet." He
chewed a piece of ice. "These people don't
let up."

"You suffer too much."

He considered this. "Suffering is the
badge of the Jewish people."

"All human beings suffer," I said.

The troutlike smile formed on his face.
"Yes, but through long practice, we Jews have
perfected the art."

Walrus stood directly in front of us. "Pardon me," he said. His white tux looked silvery under the lights. "I hope I'm not interrupting." He held out my jacket and I put it on, even though I was sweltering. I buttoned it, too. "I brought you a nice cold beer, Grace. You're not letting this fellow get you drunk on hard liquor, are you?"

I held up my glass. "Champagne."

"I wish I had a glass slipper for you to sip it from." Walrus extended one thin hand toward Malachi. "I don't believe we've been properly introduced."

"Oh, sorry!" I said. "Walrus, this is—"

"Walrus?" Malachi echoed. *"Walrus?"*

I gave him a dirty look. "This is—"

"Rabbi Ben Ezra," Malachi said, placing his empty glass in Walrus's outstretched hand. "Excuse me. It's getting dense in here." He pushed his way, hands first, into the middle of the Arena.

Walrus hoisted the glass quizzically and stared after him. "You having fun?" he asked me.

"Yes." I drank the rest of my champagne and watched Malachi weave across the Arena.

"Drinking yourself to death?" Walrus

asked, handing me the cup of beer. "I'm trying. Looks like your friend's been trying. Is
he all right?"

"He's never all right."

"I hate to see that at a party," Walrus
said. "People should enjoy themselves properly. You having fun yet?"

"Not quite yet," I said. "But I'm still
hopeful."

A young man nudged past me, splashing
half his drink on the floor next to my shoe. I
smiled brilliantly at him.

"Missed me!" I said.

He paused, off balance, resting one hand
on my shoulder, and apologized slurrily into
my face. It was Katherine's escort, without the
white turban.

"Grace," said Walrus, "this is my brother.
Justin Horssay Mattison. We call him Horsey.
This is the beautiful young lady who came
with me tonight."

The boy gave a soft moan and threw both
arms around me. The top of his head barely
grazed my chin, but he had a grip like a
young wrestler. He danced me a few steps
backward, then forward again; he was light on

his feet. After a few seconds of being rocked back and forth, I finally worked myself free.

"How do you do," I said.

Someone was breathing softly at my shoulder. "Maryanne's looking for you," Katherine told Walrus, but she kept looking at Horsey. Her eyes were shiny and dark, locked on to his. "Are you all having a good time?"

"Fine time," Horsey said. He leaned gracefully back into me. "You came all the way down on the train, Grace. That's a nice long ride, isn't it?"

"I live here in Richmond," I said.

"That was my other escort." Katherine put a delicate emphasis on the word *other*. She hadn't taken her eyes from Horsey's face.

"One thing I hate about that damned railroad," Horsey said. "They put those little flimsy white napkins behind your head to make you think they're being sanitary. But who knows what kind of old greaseball or spic's been sitting there? Makes me sick just to see them."

"Try wearing a hair net," I said.

Walrus took my arm and laughed.

"Or some old black Joe's sitting there with a chicken in his lap. Stinks to high heaven. You can't even draw a breath."

"Don't breathe," I said. "Do you happen to know where he is?" I asked Katherine. "This 'other' escort?"

Walrus grabbed my arm again. The beer sloshed around in my cup.

"Excuse me," I said. "This place stinks. I need some air." I freed my arm and walked across the room to find someplace quiet to stand. My head was pounding.

Empty peanut shells crackled under my shoes. There were plastic cups scattered around, and one woman dropped a cigarette on the floor and ground it out under her high heel. My head was buzzing. I couldn't listen to the band butcher up another Glenn Miller number, so I wandered outside to the parking lot.

It was cool out, or felt that way after the intense heat inside the Arena; pitch-black beyond the light over the door. There were couples necking in the shrubbery, making soft noises and rattling the leaves. I found a pack of cigarettes in my jacket pocket, lit one, and threw the match onto the green lawn that no longer looked green or any other color in the darkness, just another shadow laid on the first flat shadow of the evening.

The band stopped playing, and everything outside grew louder and darker. I took off my jacket and lay down on the grass.

A while later I felt a light hand on my shoulder. "Hey there," Walrus said, "are you all right?"

"I'm fine," I said. I sat up straight.

"You've got quite a temper," he said mildly.

"Do I?" I said. "Where is everyone?"

"Oh, Katherine's off consoling her poor old mama. She ripped that sad flapper dress of hers doing the Charleston." Walrus's voice floated drowsy against the silence. "You having a good time yet?"

"Sure," I said.

"Don't you really want to dance at all?"

"Not really." After a minute I added, "You go ahead, though."

"No," Walrus said. "I can't dance worth spit. Maryanne's having a good time, for once. She gets so little opportunity for pleasure. — Nor gives it," he added.

My head was still spinning. It took the bushes and trees past me in a wide circle.

"Here, have some of the dog that bit you." He handed me a plastic cup of beer. I took it and drank some.

"Go ahead and lie back down, Grace. You'll feel a lot better with your head against the earth. That's how it is with me when I've been in the heat and the noise too long."

I eased slowly, gingerly backward onto the lawn, as if the ground might slip away from me at the last second. I was conscious of Walrus sitting near me, not saying anything. Every now and then he'd shift position, or sigh, or sip his drink. After a while he got up and scraped his feet on the cement at the bottom of the stairs and sat down next to me in the grass. His shirtsleeve touched my arm, and the material was silky, like a grown man's.

When I opened my eyes the band had started up again. I heard a door bang. Someone sat down behind me. The air, which had been as light as a cloud, grew heavy.

"What is she—asleep?" a voice asked. It was Malachi, followed close behind by another bang of the door. I sat up straight.

"Never mind about her," Horsey said.

"I'm telling you, there is nothing crooked about the Southern Stock Exchange."

"Oh, right," said Malachi. "Not like the bankers and moneylenders."

"Now, now," said Walrus. "Boys, please."

"What do you do on the stock exchange, exactly?" Katherine asked.

"We make money," Horsey said, bored.

"That's a real goddamn accomplishment," Malachi sneered.

"You got an ugly New York mouth on you," Horsey said. "Anybody ever tell you that?"

"I'm not *from* New York," Malachi said with exaggerated patience.

"Would you two care for a soda to cool off?" Walrus said.

"I've got a drink," Malachi said. "Don't you worry your sweet head about us. —But I'd like to make a toast. To Katherine, our lovely hostess, the flavor of the week: *Caveat emptor!*—"

"Quit that," said Horsey. He put his arm around Katherine.

"I guess I'll go see how Maryanne is getting on." Walrus rose quickly to his feet. "Anyone coming?" He put his hand out to me.

"We're all getting on," Malachi said. "Believe me, she's not doing it any faster than the rest of us."

Walrus held out his hand to me again. "Grace?"

I could feel Malachi's stare boring into my back. "You should go dance with Maryanne," I said.

"Well, I *should*," Walrus said. "But I won't."

"Why don't *you* dance with her, if you're so goddamned worried?" Malachi sneered.

"You just watch how you talk to us," Horsey said. He was weaving up and down the lawn, his movements like a bullfighter in the ring. "Where are you from, anyway?"

"Philadelphia," Malachi said.

"Philadelphia. New York—same damned thing. You're all a bunch of—" He waved one hand in drunken disgust.

Malachi stepped closer to him. "Of what?"

Horsey looked him up and down. "Bankers."

"Bankers," Malachi echoed.

"Money people," Horsey said.

"Jews," said Malachi. He was breathing quick and light. "Why don't you just say Jew?"

"Dirty Jew," said Horsey, grinning like a wolf.

Malachi hit him so suddenly, I heard rather than saw the crack of it, like lightning. Then Horsey leaped forward, and the two of them fell, rolling, onto the grass. "Hey!" I yelled. Behind me, the screen door burst open.

"Horsey, what in hell are you doing?" Walrus hollered, high voiced.

A small crowd gathered at once, the couples flushed from the bushes, guests spilling out from the Arena. Someone pulled Malachi off Horsey.

"Let me get him!" Horsey was bobbing and weaving in place, trying to break free of the young men who held him with his arms pinned back. "You let me go!" he shouted hoarsely. "He doesn't belong here. Not for one second. He's got no business here in the first place!" He said it as "bidness."

"You people lost that fight in court a long time ago," Malachi said. "Hadn't you heard?"

Katherine hung on to Malachi's arm. "Stop it!" she said.

Malachi shook Katherine's hand off and smoothed back his hair. No one else approached him. A small crowd had gathered beside Horsey. They were still staring into the middle of the lawn, as if waiting for the next round.

"Well," Malachi said. "This must be the famous Southern hospitality we've heard so much about."

"Be quiet," said Katherine. "Will you please shut up now?"

"You'd all like that, wouldn't you?" Malachi said, staring around. His clothing was all bunched up and twisted. He looked almost hunchbacked. "But that's why there will always be the Jews. Always. You can't get rid of them. May as well give up. If not these Jews, then some other Jews—"

"Malachi, go home," Katherine said.

Malachi bent down and picked up his jacket from the grass. His shirt was green with grass stains. "Yez'm, Miz Scarlett. Your wish is my command."

"Somebody shut him up before I shoot him!" said Horsey. He seemed near tears.

Walrus, holding tight to his arm, led him back inside the Arena.

One by one the others began to drift away. Of those few who remained, gawking, I didn't recognize a single face. "Show's over," I said. I walked into the middle of the circle and helped Malachi on with his jacket, one sleeve at a time.

"I think it's time to go home now," Malachi said, his voice high and uncharacteristically mild. I recognized by the way he was standing crookedly, putting all his weight on one leg, that he was still drunk. We were standing alone together.

"I'll get the car. You certainly know how to liven up a party," I said.

"I mean *my* home, Steinberg. Where the heart is."

"All right, I'll take you to the airport."

"I don't fly," he said. "Remember? It's too late now for a train." He seemed to be waiting for something.

"You want me to call your father?"

He stared at me, his pupils enormous, leaving a thin ring of blue iris behind. He laughed. "Go right ahead," he said.

"What's your number?" I asked.

"Have you got a handkerchief?" he said. "I think my nose is bleeding."

I took out a small purse, opened it, and shook out a lace-edged handkerchief—my mother's idea. I gave it to him and stuck the purse back in my dress pocket.

He wiped his nose and mouth, then brought a small leather address book out of his jacket. "It's under *Gelb*," he said. "Joseph Gelb, attorney."

"All right."

"You can't miss it. The only other Gelb in there is me." He tipped forward and fell behind one of the shrubs.

"Come on out," I said.

He stuck out his hand and I pulled him out and let him collapse on the grass. He rolled over once, then lay still, like a dog that's been hit.

"Steinberg," he said.

"What?"

"Steinberg, Steinberg."

At the last minute he raised himself to a sitting position, waving his arms. "Call collect!" he yelled after me.

I passed the line of couples outside the Arena. No one even looked at me strangely;

I think I'd become a natural element of the party, like the band, the light fixtures. A few heads nodded hello as I passed. The necking couples seemed exposed and vulnerable now that a full moon had risen. Walrus had his arms wrapped around a dark-haired girl in a blue dress. He faced my way; she faced the side of the building, pausing as if between dances. Maryanne was nowhere in sight.

Inside the Arena, people were milling around the front door again, mostly on their way out. There must have been a hundred guests still wandering through, but the huge room looked empty now. The bar was littered with plastic glasses and loose ice cubes melting onto the bar top. Cigarette butts floated in the glasses, the paper slowly unwinding back from the filters. A bartender directed me to a row of pay phones inside the coatroom.

Mr. Gelb picked up on the first ring. I explained I was a friend of his son's and—

"What's the matter?" he said sharply. "What's wrong?"

"I'm sorry to be calling so late."

"I'm awake," Mr. Gelb said. "Where is he? What's going on?"

"He's outside. We're at a party now." There was a pause. "He drank too much, he isn't feeling well, and he wants to come home."

Mr. Gelb cleared his throat. "What is he, drunk?"

"I don't know, Mr. Gelb." This wasn't the kind of thing I was any good at. I was exhausted and I lacked practice. "Can he come home or not?"

"Here?" There was a split-second's silence. "I guess so, yes. Of course he can. Which flight?"

"Well, he won't fly, so I—"

"Shit," Mr. Gelb said. "That's right. Excuse me—Willa, is it?"

I hesitated. "Willie."

"Willie. Excuse my language. You aren't suggesting I fly there to get him, are you? Because he's eighteen years old; he's not a child."

I turned and faced the other way. The short metal loop of the pay phone stuck straight up into my face and I batted it down with my free hand.

"Is he acting crazy? How bad is he?" He didn't wait for an answer. "Would he fly if

I came down to get him? Just tell me yes or no."

"I don't know," I said.

"If I have to fly down, I'll fly down. But I want you to know you're putting a gun to my head."

"I could put him on the phone," I said. "Maybe you could talk to him."

"You're putting a gun to my head," Mr. Gelb said.

"I'm sorry. I know it's late—"

"I'm awake, goddamn it! Can you get him to the airport in D.C.? Because I'm not flying into Richmond at this hour."

"Yes," I said.

"I'll be glad to pay for your gas. Tolls. Your time, whatever."

"That's not necessary."

"Have you been drinking, too?" he asked. "Can you drive all the way to Washington?"

"I'm not drunk, sir."

"You're old enough to drive? You have a license?"

"Yes sir," I said.

He was quiet for a time, just breathing. "I'd rather fly the extra twenty minutes than put two young lives in danger."

"I can drive to Washington, Mr. Gelb."

"Give me your number there," he said. "Let me think about it. I'm calling you right back."

I gave him the number, and we both hung up. I rubbed my ear. It felt as if they had put lead in the earpiece instead of plastic. I sat down on the carpet under the row of telephones and slipped off my too-tight high heels. I spent my life wearing sneakers, and I wasn't used to wobbling two inches above the ground. The pay phones were just inside the cloakroom, and I looked around at the raincoats and wraps hanging next to me. I rested my face in my hands and closed my eyes. The phone rang over my head, and I jerked awake.

"I forgot your name," Mr. Gelb said.

"Willie Steinberg."

"All right, Miss Steinberg. Have you got a pencil and paper? There's a flight in at Dulles at one o'clock. Can you get there? You know where you're going?"

"Yes," I said. "I live here."

"You sure?"

"Mr. Gelb," I said. "Please."

"Then write this down: Flight 204, Frank-

lin Airlines. It's a small airline in a big airport." Mr. Gelb cleared his throat with a little
humming sound. "So. Are you the young
woman who composes music?"

"I guess so," I said, taken aback. How
would he know? I wondered.

He was quiet so long I thought we'd been
disconnected. "That's nice," he finally said.
"Malachi doesn't talk about his girlfriends
much, but I thought I remembered that name:
Willie. Have you two been going out long?"

"Not too long," I said. I tried to keep my
voice neutral.

"He spoke very highly of your musical
ability."

"Well, okay," I said. "I'll tell him you're
coming."

"Flight 204. Franklin Airlines. Out of
Philly."

"Got it." I made it sound as if I was writing it down. "Thanks, Mr. Gelb. We'll be seeing you."

"Thank *you*," he said, and hung up.

I slid my high heels back on mechani-
cally. All the lightness from the champagne
had turned leaden. That same instant I be-
came aware that someone was watching me,

had been watching all along. A woman—the cloakroom attendant—limped forward from behind the coatracks, smoking a cigarette. Her hair was slicked back and wet looking, as if she'd just sprayed it. She was wearing some sort of nondescript wrapper or uniform. I didn't know whether maybe I was expected to tip her. She was acting drunk.

"Are you having a nice time?" she asked. She thrust her face too close to mine. She looked exhausted and her eyes were red.

"Yes," I said. I fumbled around in my purse for a dollar.

Her voice grew more ingratiating. "What about the others?" she asked, cocking her head at the cloakroom door. "Are they all having a nice time, too?" She laid her hand on my arm.

Katherine came around the corner then. She swept past as if she hadn't seen me and went directly to the other woman. "For God's sakes, Mama, where have you been?"

"I've been right here," Mrs. Randolph said, releasing my arm. "We've just been having a little chat." She nodded at me.

I dropped the dollar bill inside my purse and closed it.

"Everyone's waiting to say good night to you," Katherine said. "Excuse us, Grace." She tucked her arm through her mother's, and they walked away, their bodies inclining toward one another as they went, as if to hold each other up.

I waited a few minutes before I headed back out. The colored lights had been switched off the dance floor, but one or two couples were still dancing cheek to cheek in the darkness. Maryanne was dancing with Mr. Randolph. Their faces were pressed close, and the light from above made them look bright and blurry, like an Impressionist painting. I walked out an emergency exit at the back, pushing down a metal bar, half expecting to set off an alarm.

Instead I stepped quietly off a three-foot drop into blackness, twisting my ankle. *"Damn,"* I said, and limped back to the dark side of the Arena.

Malachi was lying exactly where I'd left him. I nudged him with the tip of my shoe and he propped himself up on his elbows. "Was anyone home?" he asked. "They go out a lot on weekends."

"They were home."

"Did you talk to my stepmother? She sounds like Doris Day, right? Very cheerful. You should hear her sing 'Que Sera, Sera.' "

I shivered, folding my arms over my chest. The grass was wet around my ankles. "Your father's flying in to Dulles Airport. You know where that is?"

Malachi nodded. "No," he said. "My father?"

"Yes or no?"

He nodded again.

I gave up. "We'll find a map. Let's get going."

"Where are we going?" he said.

"To Dulles. Airport." I enunciated carefully, as if he were hard of hearing. "Where your father is going to meet us. Remember?"

"My father?" He tugged up handfuls of grass, trying to pull himself to a sitting position. "You mean he's coming here? What for?"

"I put a gun to his head," I said.

Malachi rose unsteadily to his feet. "You called him? You actually called my father in the middle of the night? You're crazier than I thought, Steinberg! What did he say?" He brushed frantically at his knees and pants cuffs.

"He insisted," I said, staring off at the Arena parking lot. The cars were scattered across it like pieces of pastel-colored candy. "He wanted to come. He told me you're his firstborn son, even if you are a raving lunatic, and he loves you."

Malachi straightened up and looked at me. "My father said that?"

"That's right," I said.

"He said all that to you on the phone?"

"Yes."

Malachi placed both hands heavily on my shoulders and drew me toward him, as if he was going to kiss me. Instead, he peered into my face. "Steinberg, why would you make up a crazy thing like that? What's the matter with you?"

I stared back at him. He dropped his hands from my shoulders.

"I've got to get directions," he said, pointing at me. "You. Wait here." He took a few steps forward and stumbled onto his knees. His arms went slowly out for balance. He pushed himself back off the grass and staggered sideways, like a crab. It was painful to watch him.

"I'll go," I said. "Just sit here. Sit."

Walrus escorted me out to his car. He exuded the bittersweet smell of gin from his breath, his skin, his hair; the air around us was perfumed by gin. A silver flask jutted out of his jacket pocket. Every few steps he would stop, take it out of his pocket, and offer the flask to me. "Help yourself."

"No thanks. I've had enough."

He'd take another swig as if he was drinking water. "Terrible thing, Grace. I hate to see that sort of thing at a party. I want you to know that I personally have a great fondness for you people. And I mean that sincerely. I dated a Jewish girl one time. Sorority girl—fine girl." He drank from the flask and put it away again.

I held a flashlight while he rummaged through his glove compartment. He pulled out road maps of New England and New Mexico and Colorado and western Canada, and finally produced a tattered map of Virginia from the bottom of the pile.

"Next car I'm buying," he said, lifting an

advertisement flyer and letting it fall. "Silver-gray Audi. Fox. Grace, look here."

I pointed the flashlight.

"All these maps, and I don't go any-where." His voice rose thinly and sweetly out of the darkness. "I've never even been to Wall Street. —Business. No matter what they offer you, don't you take it."

"Okay," I said.

"Okay, okay!" he echoed. "That's what *I* said. Don't you go do it." He touched my head. "Pretty hair." He slammed the glove compartment shut and slumped sideways to-ward me. " 'Scuse me." He drew himself straight. His face glimmered palely, green-ish white above the beam of the flashlight. "You're an artist," he said heavily. "That's wonderful, Grace. I'm not kidding. I'll bet you're a fine musician; sensitive. My brother Horsey's a poet. That's why he goes off that way. Otherwise they've got you married and buried and off to the races before you know what hit you. And there isn't anything on this green earth they can give you to make it up." He leaned toward me. "Am I right?"

I said that he was.

He drank from the flask. "Maryanne's a

wonderful, proper girl, Grace. Proper. I wish you'd gotten to know her better. I certainly wish *I* had. We're going to be married end of summer. You can be the maid of honor. Okay?"

"Okay," I said.

"Okay." He turned in his seat and put his hand on the side of my face. "Grace," he said. "Could I kiss you good night? Just one time?"

Before I could think of a nice or at least polite way to say no, his body leaned in slowly against me, like a sheltering tree, and every sound between us was close up and magnified. The kiss was over before I'd had the presence of mind to say anything. His body moved slowly away, shoulders and chest last. By the time he spoke again, it seemed he had walked to the far side of a bridge and it stretched between us.

"You send us a postcard from the New York Philharmonic when you get there—all right?" he said. "I know you will be. A famous magician. —Musician." He drew a pen from his breast pocket. I thought he was going to ask me for my autograph. Instead he tapped the pen on the map of Virginia. "Here's a shortcut for you, Grace. It'll get you to Dulles in no time at all."

There were now two shapes waiting by the side of the Arena. Katherine was sitting on Malachi's jacket. It was spread out underneath her like a sail.

"Where the hell were you?" Malachi asked. He was pacing in and out of the circle cast by the light above, and he looked at me with a face distorted by emotion, as if they'd been arguing.

"I wish you didn't have to leave yet," Katherine said, pulling up blades of grass from the lawn. "It's still so early."

"We had a great time," Malachi told her. "Right, Steinberg?"

"Right," I said.

Katherine tossed the handfuls of grass away. "It's so early. My mother won't sleep for days, wondering what went wrong."

"Nothing went wrong," Malachi said. "Believe me. Everyone had a wonderful time. It was a great party. Stop worrying."

She brushed her hands on her dress. They were clenched into fists. "Horsey left with his brother, I guess."

"Which brother?" I asked.

"Which *brother?*" Malachi sneered. "The one you disappeared with. The engaged one.

The one who walked around all night with his hands in your pockets."

"Oh, *that* brother."

"It's not even midnight," Katherine said.

"May I have my handkerchief back?" I asked Malachi.

"No, you may not."

I looked away, toward the sloping hill of a nearby golf course. It looked like something on another planet. Farther on was the lit gray ribbon of the highway. Trucks crawled by, like swimmers over water.

Katherine glanced from one of us to the other. "Dulles isn't that far," she said. "Don't worry. You'll get there in plenty of time."

"I'm not worried," Malachi said. "I'll get a map somewhere, I'll find it. —You look exhausted," he added. There was a gentleness in his voice I'd never heard. "Go inside, now. Your parents are looking for you, I'll bet. Don't worry. The party was great; everyone had a good time."

One instant she was smoothing her dress down over her knees with her fists and the next she was standing. Something slipped from her hand onto the ground. "Willie, it was good of you to come," she said to me.

She half turned toward Malachi. "Thank you for coming all this way," she told him. "I'm so sorry. You're a truly wonderful—a wonderful escort."

She pressed her face into his shirt, turning her head sideways against his chest. His bony wrists stuck out of his shirtsleeves as he patted her back. His neck was arched away to keep his head from resting on top of hers, his mouth stretched out widely, as I thought at first, in a smile; then I saw his eyes. I looked away.

He waited till she had walked past the line of couples, down the path, and back to the Arena, and when she turned and waved, he waved back. Then he stooped down, keeping his back stiffly to me. He picked up whatever she had been gripping in her hand and flourished it by the corner. It was my handkerchief.

"Steinberg," he intoned, handing it back to me, his mouth still stretched out in that pained smile. "In this wonderful world, let it never be said that all is lost."

Chapter Six

MALACHI DOZED on the way to the airport, his head tilted back against the car window, his legs bent sideways. He seemed to take up all the space in the car. One large hand was flung across his forehead, palm out—the gesture of an actor in a melodrama. He mumbled incoherently in his sleep, and he jerked awake with a start when I pulled onto the soft clay shoulder of one of Walrus's back-road shortcuts. "Are we okay?" he half shouted. "Are we all right?"

He unscrewed himself from his corkscrew sleeping position and peered over my shoulder at the map. "We lost?" he asked.

"No," I said irritably. "Go back to sleep."

I wasn't sure if we were really lost or not. I wasn't sure I cared, either. All I wanted was to get this over with, get rid of Malachi, drive home, and go to bed. Walrus's spidery scrawl required a leap of faith every time I made a turn, and I had stopped in the middle of nowhere to consult the map again. We were parked at the crest of a low hill, on some narrow, numberless two-lane highway between dark, wide-stretching fields. A few feet back from the road was an old-fashioned street lamp; a few yards farther back lay a country graveyard. The gravestones flashed like haunted-house mirrors in the reflection from my headlights.

One large monument stood guard nearest the road, with a statue on top, an angel poised forward like a runner, wings half spread.

"You must have been having nightmares," I told Malachi. "You were talking up a storm."

"Yeah?" he said, interested. "What did I say?"

"I don't know. I wasn't taking notes."

He yawned so widely his jaw cracked. "Well, next time pay attention. I'll say something profound." He tugged at his collar and the elastic bow tie came off in his hand. He looked at it, then opened the glove compartment and put it inside. "Here. A small token of my esteem." He rubbed a clear circle on the car window and looked out. "I'm going to go stretch my legs."

"Don't take too long."

"It's a euphemism, Steinberg." He opened the car door and left it open. Cool air rolled in from the dark field as if off a lake.

I held the map up to the diffused, distant light of the street lamp, located the thin black line that marked the back road I thought we were on, outlined it heavily in pencil, then went over the route to the airport three times to make sure I had it right. Ten or fifteen minutes passed. When I looked back out through the open car door, Malachi was nowhere in sight; just the big stone angel hovering over me, angling toward the graves.

I honked the car horn. The sound blasted the air, then thinned out over the fields on either side.

"Come on out here," Malachi called to me from somewhere near the graves. "It's peaceful where I am."

No other cars had passed since we'd stopped. The place felt eerie, and not just because of the graves. The leaves on the trees showed their glimmering silver-gray undersides, like fish swimming through the mist. He hooted, imitating an owl.

"Malachi!" I yelled. "Let's go. This is creepy."

"It's homey," he said. "Trust me."

One tiny light flickered on and off in the long grass, and after a few seconds there were three or four blinking, then dozens of them. The flashes looked like coded messages against the graves or sparks flying off the telephone wires. Fireflies were everywhere. "Where are you?" I called.

"Under these trees. What are they called, anyway?"

"I think they're cypress," I said, getting out of the car and heading blindly toward the sound of his voice. "Keep talking."

"They can't be cypress. Cypress are evergreen, aren't they? These have big black leaves."

"I don't know, then," I said. I stumbled on one high-heeled shoe—it was the ankle I had twisted earlier—and clutched at a tilting gravestone, slick with dew. "Ask the forest ranger."

"Where's he buried? Heh heh." Malachi sat overlooking the graves, his back propped against a tree trunk. The moon was so bright I could see him clearly. He'd taken off his coat and folded it into a square he was sitting on. "Always maintain a respectable distance from the dead," he said. "It's never going to be far enough. You need a hand?" He reached for me as I climbed the slippery, grass-covered slope. I waved him off.

"Sit on my jacket," he said.

"No thanks." I remained standing.

"Okay, so what's with your father," he said. "Is he in the CIA? Or what? What's the big mystery?"

I folded my arms over my chest. "Let's get going, Malachi. It's late and I'm tired."

"In a minute," he said sharply. "I'm trying to have a pleasant conversation. How'd you like the party? Did you fall for that rich stockbroker?"

"Don't be a jerk."

"You don't confide in me much, Steinberg."

"I don't tell anyone much."

"No kidding," he sneered. "I thought you were an open book. I thought you wore your heart on your big empty sleeve, you self-righteous Amazon."

"I'm going now," I said. "You can come along or not."

He turned his hands over in his lap and studied them. "You're not even human, Steinberg. You know that? You've got no soul. You don't know anything about love. You're a freak! A *stone*. You invited me down here just so you could watch the peep show. There's nothing inside you! No heart. That's why your music isn't worth the flimsy paper it's written on."

I started to walk away. "Why don't you make your freaking speeches to the moon?"

"Hey!" he shouted. "I'm not done talking to you." He cut in front of me, blocking my path. "I'm just getting started," he said hoarsely.

I pushed him out of my way. He stepped aside, then caught me by the arm, pulling me around to face him. "Tell me. What do you plan to do?" he said. "Stay home and live with your mother? I've got news for you,

Steinberg: She doesn't need you hanging around. I don't even think she *wants* you. I'm warning you. You're going to end up working alone behind some fast-food counter somewhere, as big as a school bus."

He said something else after that, but all I heard was a dull roar, and Malachi was somewhere behind it, still jabbering, saying things. Everything got mixed up in my head.

The next thing I knew I had grabbed him by the front of his shirt, the fabric bunched in my hands. "Let me alone! You crazy son of a bitch, you're the one who's hopeless. Look at you! In another five years they'll have you put away. They'll have you locked up where you belong!" I punctuated everything I said by punching him on the shoulders and chest, hitting him till my hands ached.

"That doesn't hurt," he kept saying. "That's nothing—I can't even feel it!" His skin was greenish white, but he kept grinning into my face. I aimed my fist for the center of his forehead and smashed him as hard as I could with the side of my hand. I think I hit his nose instead. It felt like I'd broken my wrist.

"Are you done?" he gasped, still smiling at me between gritted teeth.

"No!" I shook him so hard his teeth rattled. "How did I get stuck with you? Tell me. I can't stand you! What did I do to deserve you? What did I do wrong?" I shook him again, but his eyes were closed.

"Let me go," he said quietly.

I let go and stepped back. My legs were trembling so hard I didn't think I could stay standing on my feet, but I managed to limp away and sit down heavily in the weeds. The palms of my hands were stinging. Malachi sat a few feet away, his head down, wheezing. Neither of us spoke for a few minutes. I pulled up blades of grass and let them fall.

"Are you okay?" I said finally.

"Yes. Sure," he said stiffly. He was looking off into the distance. "I'm perfect." He stirred, sat up straight, and took something out of his pocket wrapped in a white napkin.

"What's that?"

"A biscuit. I took it from the party," he said, carefully unwrapping it. "You want some? It's good."

"No," I said.

"By the way, that diamond ring—"

"Forget it."

"I threw the ring away," he said, his mouth full.

"You did?"

He didn't answer, but kept chewing with his mouth open.

"You're drunk, aren't you?"

"Not really." He thought about it. "Not drunk enough."

"Where did you throw it?"

He gestured with the biscuit. "Somewhere back at the Arena. In the bushes. I don't know, I wasn't looking."

"I'll bet somebody finds it."

"Let them. It was a cheap ring anyway. Go back and look for it yourself, Steinberg, if you want it that badly." He held the biscuit between both hands, lifted his shoulders, and took another bite. "You sure you don't want this? It's good."

"What is it—a ham biscuit?"

"Ham?" His jaw stopped moving.

I tried to take it back. "Never mind," I said.

He spat the mouthful into his napkin and covered it up. "What? What did you call this?"

"Nothing. Forget it. —It's just an expression."

"An *expression?* What kind of an expression is *ham biscuit?*" He clutched the napkin. "Oh God," he said thickly. "I just ate ham."

"Well, you didn't exactly—"

"Shut up!" He threw the napkin into the darkness. I watched it arc away, white. He stumbled a few feet away. "Ham. I'm going to be sick."

"You're not," I said.

"What the hell do you know about it?" he said.

I got to my feet. "Take it easy."

"Why did I come here? Why? Oh God!" he groaned.

I edged closer and touched his shoulder. "Hey. Malachi."

"I don't want your pity!" He jerked away as if he'd been burned. "Stay away from me, Steinberg, I'm warning you!" He shook off my hand and lurched off in the direction of the graves. One minute he was standing at the edge of what looked like a small cliff, overlooking the graveyard, and the next instant he stepped off, like a cartoon character. I watched him fall. A few seconds later he rose up soundlessly, though it looked like he should have broken his neck. His white shirt appeared and disappeared rapidly between the dark stones.

I followed, skidding down a wet grassy hill. My ankle turned sideways and one of the high heels snapped off altogether. I kept on going without the shoes. I couldn't see him anywhere.

There was a rustling sound down by the big stone monument. I spotted something that looked like a white blur. Malachi had settled something on top of his head and he swayed back and forth, striking himself in the chest. Now and again his head slipped forward and bumped against the stone angel. It looked like he was praying to it.

"What are you doing?" I whispered.

A few feet away I stopped. The air smelled brackish and sour. He stood bent like a question mark. He straightened sharply, raising one hand as if in warning, then doubled over at the waist with a wet hacking sound. I backed up a few steps. "Are you okay?"

He took the thing off his head—it was my

handkerchief—and dabbed his mouth. "Excuse me," he said, placing the handkerchief carefully back on his head. He propped one hand against the stone, leaning all his weight against it. There was a dull thud every time he smacked his head against it. *"Ashamnu,"* he chanted. *"Bagadnu, gazalnu."* I remembered the Jewish prayer. *I have sinned, I have betrayed, I have stolen.*

I snatched the handkerchief off his hair and threw it into the grass. "Let's get out of here," I said. "Come on."

He butted his head again, without looking up. "Just leave me alone. All right?"

I moved in a little closer and laid the back of my hand against the granite stone, cupping my palm so that my hand was between him and the monument. He rammed his head into my hand and looked up, surprised. "Nice trick," he said.

After a few seconds he let go of the angel. "My mother had a lousy love life, that's why I'm so screwed up. —You can take your hand away now."

Around us were all the old country graves, barely visible by the light of the one lone street lamp. I tilted back my head and started counting stars. Sometimes that helped to distract me, but out in the graveyard the sky looked far off and immense, as if you could fall through the black spaces ·between the stars. I stopped, dizzy and motion sick. Malachi was looking at me, eyes shining like an animal's in the dark, his head cocked.

"You know about the thirty-six virtuous souls, don't you, Steinberg?" he said. "From Jewish mysticism. We don't know who they are, or where, but they're around on earth someplace. For the sake of those thirty-six, God keeps things going. That's the tradition. But I think there's one more." He leaned in closer. "A cosmic orphan. The messenger." It was too dark to tell, but it looked like his nose was bleeding. "He holds God accountable."

I looked away from the blood. "For what?"

"For the dead." Malachi's arm shot out and his hand gripped my wrist like a vise.

My heart gave a frightened jump. "Quit kidding around," I said.

"Some joke, huh, Steinberg?" He tilted his head toward the graves. "That's the little joke someone's going to tell on you one of these days." He let go of my wrist. "Right there, six feet down. The funny bones. The dead are helpless, Steinberg. They need someone to protect them. A guardian. *Tikkun olam*—someone to make reparations."

"Malachi," I said. "Your nose is bleeding."

He shook his head impatiently, wiping his nose with the back of his hand, smearing the blood. "I can't stand this world. I hate the whole stinking thing. It's unbearable, living on this side of time." He lowered his voice, touching my arm. "My mother was in two of the Nazi death camps," he said. "Treblinka and Auschwitz. Did you know that?"

"I heard something about it."

"That's right," he said. "They injected a pint of orange juice into her little brother's arm so afterward it never bent forward or back. They pulled out people's fingernails and toenails. They made children bathe in filthy, frozen water, gave them experimental injections, and when they were done with all that they led them all into little cement bunkers and gassed them. Or threw them directly into the ovens—to save on gas. My God! My God!" He let out a hoarse cry. "You think He's in on this? Where was He, thirty, forty years ago? Where is He, ever? It's all in the past, right?" His voice cracked. "I know how I look to you, Steinberg, I'm not stupid. But I refuse to forget. I just don't think we can pretend this never happened, that this kind of slaughter isn't always happening, that it's not happening right now, this minute, somewhere—"

"Malachi." I hesitated a minute. "Wait. That suit, the ring . . . You mean you did it on purpose? Your father didn't buy you that getup, did he? He wouldn't be caught dead letting you wear something like that."

"He didn't have to buy it. It was in our attic," he said. Malachi touched one hand to his forehead. "I'm not crazy," he said. "I just have a long memory. Things keep disappearing off the face of the earth. Somebody has to try and keep it alive, all those people." He dropped his hand from his face. "Look, I would die for them, if I could. I would be extremely happy to die."

It was still and bright in front of the graves. The clouds had suddenly parted, and the moon shone lower in the sky, as if drawn down by the silver flecks of mica glittering in the stones.

Malachi turned one of his hands over on

the ground, palm up. His fingers, I saw in that instant, were covered with blood: even his fingertips, palms, the skin between his fingers. Everything was bloody.

"Stand up," I said. His hair was matted with pinkish red clots of blood. The front of his shirt was a gory mess, like something out of a horror movie. There was already a graveyard odor around him. My heart was pounding so hard in my chest I thought I was going to faint.

I put my arms tightly around him, as if by holding him hard enough I could hold back the blood. It was slippery and cool in his hair, like clay, and smelled like clay, and then I grabbed his shoulders and leaned back and stared into his face till it finally hit me it really *was* clay—the red clay soil of Virginia. I started laughing.

"What is it?" he asked. "What's the matter with you?"

I laughed till I thought I was going to be sick. I stood up and walked around in a circle for a minute. The ground was cold and wet under my feet, and I didn't understand why. I looked down and saw I was standing in my stocking feet.

"Your zhuse," he said.

"What?"

He pointed at my feet. "Your zhuse. Damn." He reached up and touched his top lip gingerly. It was swollen and his speech slurred around it. *"Shoes."*

"They're back on that hill somewhere."

"I'll go get them," he said. "You wait here."

I nodded, staring at the ground. Tears were sliding down my face, and I turned my head away. I didn't know why I was crying. Tears kept falling and stinging against my cheeks, and the ground was so wet and cold my teeth were chattering.

"Put this on," Malachi said, coming up behind me. He dropped his black jacket over my shoulders. The fabric was heavy and coarse as canvas sacking, with a damp, musty smell. He handed me my shoes and I put them on. I tried to hand the jacket back.

"It's warm, at least. Come on, Steinberg. Put it on."

I poked my arm through the sleeves. The jacket smelled like a mixture of ancient mothballs, stale tobacco, and dust.

He touched my elbow. "Check the inside pocket, Steinverg. There's something I want you to have."

"No thanks," I said.

His white shirt glowed in the moonlight. "Just check the pocket." He folded his arms across his chest. "Go on. Look."

I reached one hand gingerly inside and my fingers bumped against what felt like a stone. I lifted it out and a short chain slithered after.

"It's a watch." Malachi was studying me closely, his expression unreadable. "My grandvather's. It opens. Go ahead, open it."

"Is this some kind of trick?" I said.

He just looked at me. The watch felt heavy in the palm of my hand, like something that had lain underwater a long time. The top of the watch was flat as a quarter, but the bottom was smoothly rounded. When I pressed a tiny lever at the side, the top flew up, revealing an elegant watch face with spidery hands. I shut it and turned the watch over. I could feel engraving with my fingertips but couldn't make out the writing.

"It says, 'Time is money,'" Malachi told

me. "My grandvather was a capitalist in the deepest sense. The top is made out of a five-dollar gold piece."

"It's beautiful."

"Well, anyway," he said. "It's yours."

"Oh no." I tried to hand it back. "I can't take this. I mean, I appreciate the gesture and all—"

"It's not a *gesture*," Malachi said. "It's a gift. For you."

"No, I really can't—"

"Just take the goddamn thing," he said. "For once in your life, accept something gracefully."

I bent my head to look at the watch. It ticked in my hand, like a live thing, the heart of a mouse. "Well, okay," I said slowly. "Thanks. Thank you."

When he smiled, his upper lip was swollen so it showed all his front teeth, like a wolf. I hated thinking I had done that. He was sagging against the monument; he looked terrible.

"It's getting late," I said tentatively.

"Yeah."

"You okay?" I asked.

"Sure." His face was pinched and yellow, and a lump was forming on his forehead. He touched it gingerly. "Old army injury. Always acts up in bad weather."

I limped forward on my broken high heel and stood next to him.

After a few seconds, he leaned his arm on my shoulder. I put my arm gingerly around his waist. We held ourselves stiffly upright, leaning away so no other part of us touched. We walked back out to the road that way, very slowly, listing sideways a little as we went. If there had been a car coming in either direction we would have certainly been hit. His car door still hung open, dimly lit and cavernous against the edge of the field. I leaned my body against the car and watched Malachi slide his legs inside. I took off his jacket and handed it to him. Then I got in and started the engine.

"Lucky we didn't burn out the battery," I said.

He nodded. His upper lip almost touched the bottom of his nose, and it was flecked with blood. He angled himself in the seat to face me, shifting his legs around. "Vy the way," he said. Something about his tone of voice made me look up. He paused, staring at his hands. "My mother wasn't in a concentration camp. Actually." He glanced over at me, then quickly back down. "I made it up, from things I read. She died in the Bronx, of stomach cancer." He tipped his head back against the seat and shut his eyes. "The trouble with history: it's a forced march. You're trapped in it. You can't look back, you can't look forward, except at the head of the person right in front of you. —And everywhere you go, you're stepping over the bodies."

I turned on the headlights of my father's car. The brights came on, dazzling the dark swell of road ahead. I flicked them off, staring at the next rise. It looked unreal, like a brightly painted scene set. "I'm sorry," I said. "About everything I said back there."

Malachi reached over and rested his hand lightly on the back of my neck. He pretended he wasn't doing it, and I pretended I didn't notice. After a minute, he took his hand away. "It's okay," he said. "Anyway, you were right. I *am* crazy."

I pulled the car back onto the road, steering carefully, keeping the palm of one hand flat on Walrus's map. The car fishtailed and swayed onto the highway, then straightened.

"Maybe so," I said. "But you're the best friend I've got."

Chapter Seven

Mr. Gelb was sleeping in the darkened lounge of the Franklin Airways terminal, slumped against the wall on a gold upholstered bench. His eyes were shut, one hand was clamped around a newspaper folded into fourths, commuter style, on his thigh. He wore a short-sleeved yellow sport shirt unbuttoned at the throat.

Malachi and I stood in the corridor a few feet outside the gate, watching him through the Plexiglas window as if he were on TV. There was nothing else to see. The commuter end of the airport was deserted at that hour; half the arrival and departure boards shut down for the night.

There was a makeshift red Franklin Airways counter set up just outside the lounge, and a fat, elderly employee stood behind it, his belly bulging out of a scarlet jacket with gold wings on each shoulder. His head was lowered so that his chin almost touched his chest. He looked dead on his feet. At the sound of our footsteps he rocked forward, as if we'd shaken him awake. "You all on this flight?" he asked.

Malachi nodded reluctantly. I took a step back.

"That your father in there?" He tapped a stack of red luggage tags against the plywood counter and looked at me.

"Let me look again," Malachi said. "Yes. That's him."

"Go on ahead, now," said the man, riffling through some paperwork. "Malkee. Right. I've already checked your tickets through."

Malachi hung back. Under the fluorescent lights, his disheveled red hair looked greenish, and his upper lip was swollen to twice its normal size. "I hate these small flanes," he told me. Everything he said came out pained and emphatic, his lip curled away from his teeth.

"Small planes are the safest," I said.

Malachi glanced across the way at his father, sleeping. "Didn't Ben Franklin fly a kite in the middle of a thunderstorm? What kind of a safety record is that?" His face looked thin and sallow; his freckles stood out in coppery blotches.

The man behind the counter stared at his feet. A woman screamed, tinnily, and there was a burst of gunfire around our knees. Malachi made an involuntary noise. The man looked up from his television. "*Boarding*," he said.

"Go ahead," I told Malachi. "I'll see you around, okay? I'll see you."

The ticket man drew him into the lounge, steering him by the arm, and I backed up a few steps into the corridor, hoping to avoid a long farewell. I would rather just drop dead than have to say good-bye.

But Malachi was already striding toward his father, quickly, like a young boxer heading into the ring. He leaned forward and touched his father on the shoulder, and Mr. Gelb startled upright. I couldn't hear what they were saying. Mr. Gelb stood, and his newspaper skidded off his thigh onto the gold carpet. He pressed one large hand on either side of Malachi's head and put his lips to the disheveled red hair, then his forehead, as if checking for fever. He leaned back suddenly, gripping Malachi's shoulders. They both began to argue and gesticulate.

Malachi shrugged. He turned and beckoned to me impatiently, tapping his fingers against the heel of his hand. His suit was caked with red mud. His shoes were filthy, too, and cracked in a dozen places. I sidled forward. I knew I didn't look much better.

"What *happened?*" Mr. Gelb asked his son.

"We had 'a change a tire," Malachi said, turning his head to look at me.

"Into what?" Mr. Gelb lowered his heavy eyelids, studying his son, then smiled a thin smile that turned down sharply at the corners. He finally glanced in my direction, lifted his eyebrows, and nodded, as if he'd spotted me that second. I felt myself slump down.

"You must be Willie, right? Thanks. Thank you for coming." He hesitated, then reached out and shook my hand. "The two of you. What happened—you had a blowout?" he asked slyly.

"A 'lat tire," Malachi said. "Do we have to discuss it?"

"Nah. Forget it." Mr. Gelb rubbed his temples with the outstretched fingers of one hand. "Our plane leaves at one-twenty. What time is it now?"

I checked my wristwatch. "Almost ten of one," I said.

"That gives us some time to kill. If there's anything open."

Malachi rolled his eyes.

Mr. Gelb frowned suddenly, and tugged at Malachi's lapel. "What is this? Where's that beautiful new suit we bought? The Calvin Klein."

"It's 'acked," said Malachi.

"What?"

" *'Acked.*"

"*What?*"

"It's packed," I said. "I can mail it back tomorrow."

Mr. Gelb let his eyes snap shut for a second, like a china doll, then flicked them open. "Send it COD," he said.

I stooped and picked up his newspaper from the carpet—it was a *Philadelphia Inquirer*—and handed it to him. The bottom of my dress was stained black almost to the knee. I felt like an overgrown flower stuck in potting soil. Mr. Gelb took the Philadelphia paper and laid it on the gold bench. "I didn't fly here at one in the morning to pick fights," he said. "I'm too goddamn tired." He snuck a look at me. "How many fathers do you know, Willie, who would come running after their kids, *mitten derinnen*—in the middle of nowhere, at this hour? Not too goddamn many, I bet."

"No sir."

Mr. Gelb studied my face with a bemused expression. I studied his. He looked away. "Yeah, well, I'm crazy to do it at all," he said. Down the corridor, an old black man navigated an institutional-size vacuum cleaner, stepping carefully back and forth over the hose as he worked. The enormous vacuum cleaner looked like some sea monster he was wrestling. The whole corridor had an undersea look—dark blue carpet, small lights high up on the walls like portholes.

Mr. Gelb consulted his own watch. "Look. We've got twenty-six minutes to kill. You want a bite to eat? There's got to be a coffee shop."

"I really should get going," I said.

"Have a cup of coffee, at least. It'll keep you awake. You've got a long haul back."

"Thanks. I don't drink coffee."

Mr. Gelb glanced at me with those hooded eyes. He looked at Malachi. "She doesn't drink coffee? What kind of an American is she? What *does* she drink?"

Malachi shrugged uncomfortably.

Mr. Gelb's turned-down mouth was somewhere between a smile and a grimace. He regarded his son with a long, pained look. "So," he said at last. "Tell me. —What is it you want? Do you want us to spend more time together—is that it? You want to start seeing that shrink again?"

"Not now," Malachi said, flapping one hand. His face rose above the stained white collar of his shirt like a priest's; swollen, unearthly, and glum.

"I could wait with you by the gate," I offered.

"Fine!" Mr. Gelb pronounced it as if he were closing a business deal. He clapped one hand on my back and the other on Malachi's and began steering us toward the door leading onto the plane.

The Franklin Airways employee hurried

over and took his place by what looked like a small wooden podium. He blocked the doorway. "Boarding!" he cried. "Get you on early," he said.

"Fine." Mr. Gelb stepped up, glancing around to see if he was cutting in front of anyone. No other passenger was in sight. A round cardboard medallion hung above Mr. Gelb's head, decorated with a silhouette of Ben Franklin—bald top and long hair at the sides—with a gold eagle posed on his shoulder ready to strike.

"I hate this," Malachi said, practically into my ear. "I hate flying." His face looked thinner and pointier than I'd ever seen it. "If God wanted us to fly, he wouldn't have invented plane crashes."

"You'll be fine," I said. "These small aircraft are very safe."

"Sure, sure." Malachi glanced all around the room, blinking rapidly. There were sharp lines at the corners of his mouth. "If the plane goes down, write me a requiem. Keep the Calvin Klein suit."

A dull roaring started up outside. Two immense headlights glared in our direction, dazzling the waiting area. Malachi flinched.

The plane inched toward the dark glass, as if getting ready to push the building aside with its silver nose.

Mr. Gelb swung around at the roped-off entrance. "Let's go, Malachi! I don't want to miss this plane."

"I'll be right there." He looked away from me, across the waiting room. "I was thinking," he started. "You want to come with us?"

"What for?" I said.

Malachi looked me over. He raised his eyebrows and shrugged. "I don't know." He tugged at his lower lip, grimacing. "Well, the plane's not full," he said.

I laughed.

Mr. Gelb took a few rapid half-running steps back toward us through the door with his palm outstretched, as if to shake my hand through the air, and gave a short wave instead. "Let's go, Malachi! Now. I want to sleep in my own sweet bed tonight." He flapped his hand at me again. "Willie, thank you. You want some money? Here—take some money." He dug one hand into his pocket.

"No! No, thank you," I said.

"Well, send a bill for the gas, at least.

And the cleaning bill for your dress. Malachi, make sure she sends a bill!"

"It was nice meeting you," I called. The ticket man was staring longingly toward the ticket counter and TV up front.

Malachi pulled his dark blue Communist cap out of some pocket and fitted it down over his forehead, adjusting the brim. "You could think about applying to Juilliard next year," he said. "Or Rochester—that's not far from Columbia." He looked left, then right, like a ballplayer getting ready to run. He gripped my hands between both of us. He took a breath, forcing his swollen lips together. "Think about it," he said. Then he leaned forward and sharply, awkwardly, kissed me on the mouth.

"I'll call you," he said, dropping my hand. "You'll hear from me. I'll be in touch." He wheeled around and strode after his father without looking back, flinging one arm up as he went in a quick, dismissive gesture of farewell.

"Call me!" I yelled after him, a second too late—he'd already turned the corner.

The man at the gate trailed me back up

front, holding on to some papers. The TV was playing again. He stopped long enough to draw me a map of the airport and airport parking lot on the inside of a Stuckey's matchbook. As soon as I walked away, the lights in the Franklin Airways terminal shut down behind me. I stopped and took off my high heels, leaving them in an empty Delta Airlines lounge, and walked the rest of the way in my stocking feet. The old black man was still standing there in the darkness, vacuuming, leaning over the machine, eyes fixed on the tiny flickering orange light at the front of the humming vacuum. I never heard the plane take off.

The airport corridor swung out in front of me like one of those fun-house tunnels that try to knock you off your feet. There was a ladies' room off the hall, and I slipped inside to wash up. I could see myself reflected only from the shoulders up, but the bottom of my dress was still wet with dew from the graveyard grass, and the thin material clung to my legs. I dried my hands and face on some rough paper towels and walked into the night air.

It was strange to step outside without

shoes: the asphalt felt soft and tacky under-
foot. If I hadn't been disoriented already, this
would have been enough to make me feel as
if I'd landed on another planet. I crept up and
down the parking aisles, one after another,
clutching the Stuckey's matchbook map in my
hand, but I couldn't find my car anywhere. It
had simply vanished. I'd spot a car that
looked right from a distance, but when I got
close it would be the wrong model or the
wrong color altogether—orange or maroon instead of red. The sky overhead was a shimmering yellow gray from all the fluorescent
lamps in the parking lot, and maybe even
from Washington, D.C., thirty miles away. The
air didn't feel or smell Southern anymore. I
was a long way from home, and somehow I'd
lost my car. After twenty minutes or so of
dogged searching, my flowered jacket was
soaked through with sweat.

I stopped and leaned against an old
Chevy van, its metal hood cool to the touch.
I felt for the pocket watch Malachi had given
me and made out that it was already 2:40 in
the morning. I was so tired and dizzy, nothing
else seemed to matter. That same second I
remembered I had driven my father's Buick

from the party instead of my mother's car, and
then I found it right away. I was hanging on
to the last worn-out scraps of myself. If I let
go there in the airport parking lot, I was afraid
I would disappear.

I paid a dollar to a girl reading a comic
book inside her lit-up booth at the airport exit
and headed onto Route 95. Trucks roared
past me with a black wind, the vibration from
the semis rattling the Buick windows. Their
red taillights glowed like sparks and disappeared. The car felt as thin as a shell. At each
bend in the road, trees and grass loomed up,
flat and bright as a stage scrim, till at the next
curve, the vision would detach itself from the
headlights and float off sideways, sinking
down to a black void.

My father's dusty pharmaceutical leaflets
were scattered on the floor under my feet; an
old, half-empty sample box rattled in the
backseat. The car wobbled left and right under my hands. I fumbled blindly for the cassette deck under the dash and turned it on.

Out of the pitch-black dark and silence,
a small green light blinked on, and Beethoven's violin concerto drifted out of the speakers like something let down by ropes. I

recognized the tape I'd bought for my father's birthday five or so years earlier, when I was in junior high school. It sounded scratchy and old. Maybe it had always sounded that bad. It was one of those cheap recordings produced by a small, disastrous orchestra in Central Europe. The notes wobbled off-key, just the way I remembered. It made me think of what Malachi had said—how terrible it would be if time really *were* fluid and you could just be washed back into the past, or carried forward into the future on a tidal wave.

I hated the idea. I didn't want to be Grace Willa Steinberg for all eternity; once was enough. The guidance counselors in school were always talking about an identity crisis. But as far as I was concerned, *having* an identity was a lifelong crisis I wanted to get over with. Even the saddest things in life were bearable if you thought you were going through them for the last time. Music was my proof that someone else had been there before; it wasn't all quicksand—at least there were footsteps.

The Beethoven dragged out stubborn and slow, pushing through each warped note with an effort. The first violin clung to the upper line where it should have yielded to the milder second violin, not to mention the French horns and drums. The tempo played like a funeral march, and every tenth note was a quarter-tone flat. I jabbed the cassette button and the tape ejected with a protesting squawk.

The car was dense now with the sound of rushing wind, but the violin concerto went on playing in my head, unwinding like a huge spool of thread, order against chaos, ease against suffering. It went along as the car dipped and rose over the curves in the highway, bending with every twist or dip in the road, debating, arguing, trying to be persuasive, taking first Mozart's side, then Beethoven's, because it had somehow become a debate between those two, over some piece of music I'd never heard before—and the musical dream argument went on and on, almost without me, just as the car seemed to steer itself along the highway, heaving and billowing over low-rolling fog.

The new music came from a long way off, like those late-night recordings out of Rochester. It began like frozen water from a pump:

chilly and sweet, rusty and slow. Finally I
realized that it was mine. I heard clearly in
my head the first three measures I'd found in
the trash basket, played on something child-
ish and reedy, like a Flutophone. The same
three measures, mile after mile, birdlike and
rapid, till I had them by heart. The dark
chords rumbled underneath, but it was like
looking off into clouds on a summer's day—
they seemed too far away to be real. The music grew louder. It slipped on toward the edge
of a ravine. Darker music lay boiling below.
I could feel it waiting there as if someone or
something had caught me by the throat, and
I tried to imagine looking down, creeping to
the very edge where the roaring lay hidden.
Then I jerked awake, hitting my chin on the
steering wheel, my heart slamming because I
thought I'd driven off the road. In front of me,
caught in the glare of the headlights, a small
animal was dying, writhing near a ditch. A
gust of wind blew up, and the animal turned
into a paper bag that wrinkled and blew away.

I let a few trucks pass by me, roaring into
the blackness, and then saw the corrugated
steel roof of Richmond's Bristol Steel, the
familiar giant metal sculpture of the Philip

Morris pack of cigarettes, and a worn-out bill-
board for Aunt Sara's Pancake House. A few
miles later I crossed the Richmond city limit,
taking the first exit off the highway onto
Broad, looking for someplace to eat. I was
famished.

The buildings hunched gray and humble
over the web of streets, and it had begun to
drizzle. I drove past industrial smokestacks
and blacked-out gas stations, liquor stores
with padlocks on the doors. At the corner of
Broad and Jackson I read the time and temperature sign of the First Federal Bank of Virginia—several degrees cooler and five minutes
earlier than it really was. A few predawn ris-
ers were out waiting for buses, wearing single-
color uniforms, no raincoats or umbrellas.
Others seemed to be just ending their evening. A black couple ran laughing down the
street, a newspaper held slanted over their
heads. Men and women sat in a row behind
the window of an all-night diner. I was the
only white person around.

I turned the car around at a statue of Bo-
jangles, the corner of what used to be called
the Freedom Block, and drove back down
Broad Street till I found a White Tower ham-

burger place open. There was one customer inside and two workers. I went in and asked for a hamburger.

The kid behind the counter looked at me as if I were crazy. "You want one hamburger?" he asked.

"Yes," I said. "Please."

An older worker came up from behind him to peer at me. "We only sell them by the bag," he said. "Half dozen, dozen." He walked away into a back room.

The single other customer was a brown-skinned woman in a nurse's uniform. She slid her change off the counter into the palm of her hand and dropped the change into the waist pocket of her uniform. She glanced down at my stocking feet, then back at my face. "The hamburgers are real small," she said. She opened the paper bag and held it open toward me. "See?"

They looked like tiny little doughnuts and smelled like a barbecue pit. "Okay," I said. "I'll take half a dozen."

"Something to drink?" the kid asked.

"No thanks," I said, only because I hadn't had time to read the menu hanging on a white board behind him and he seemed impatient.

He stood with his back to me, tossing the hamburgers, all wrapped up, into a bag. His hands were so dark they looked navy blue. The woman went out, and a bell over the doorsill rang softly as the door opened and shut. "Okay," I added, as if he had pressed me on it. "I'll have a Coke."

"What size?" he asked, doubling over the top of the bag.

"Small," I said.

He smiled. I wasn't sure if it was the idea of someone my size ordering anything small, or something less personal. As he rang up the sale he asked, "This the first time you've eat these?"

I nodded.

"Okay," he said reassuringly. "You'll want ketchup." He dropped three packets into my hand. "Must be your first time in Richmond. You'll accustom yourself to it."

I wolfed down all six hamburgers right in the White Tower parking lot, took three or four sips of the slightly flat, very sweet Coke, and then headed home, driving with the paper cup between my feet and the greasy paper bag in my lap. The old woman's house at the corner of Gardenia and Harve was all lit up for

a party. A white van was sitting in her driveway, with a City of Richmond seal painted on
the side. No other cars were around; maybe
all the other partygoers had taken taxis. I
parked outside her house, got out of the
Buick, and closed the door, holding the
paper cup of Coke in one hand. The curb's
edge was sharp under my stocking feet, and
I stumbled as if I had not expected to touch
solid earth.

Two men were walking down her front
porch ramp, carrying something wrapped in
silvery cellophane that looked like a big musical instrument, a bass viol. They startled
when they saw me, as if I'd happened upon
two burglars. The old woman's sweet, decay-
ing flowery scent rose around me from her
shrubbery.

"Morning," the first man said. "Are you a
relative?"

"I'm a neighbor." After a second I added,
"Why?"

The other man cleared his throat. "Just
let us get by with her a minute, will you."

They hurried past, carrying the thing
wrapped up in silver foil and opened and shut
the double doors at the back of the van.

"She went a few hours ago," said the tall man.

"Went where?" I asked. The question echoed back along the driveway down to where I was standing in the street in my stocking feet, still holding on to my cup of blackish brown soda.

"We've been trying to locate somebody to identify her," he said. "Any friends, or relations."

"We're new here," I said. "Me and my family. That's where I live," I added, pointing at my house across the way.

They both looked at me.

"Could you possibly identify her?" he asked. The other man unlocked the back of the van and opened the double doors, as if they'd decided to put my neighbor back inside her house, safe and sound.

"They'll keep her in the morgue till someone shows up, elsewise. Could take a while," he added.

I let this sink in, and I was sorry, so sorry—I wanted to drop to my knees in the middle of the street, apologize to the dead old woman for treating her like a drunk. She had loved music—she had loved even my mu-

sic—and that made her more of my compa-
triot than anyone else in the entire city of
Richmond.

The taller man took off his cap—his hair
was iron gray underneath and cropped short,
military style. He and the other man wore
blue plastic identification badges clipped on
the fronts of their white jackets, which jingled
when they moved. "Would you mind stepping
over here a minute?"

"All right," I said. My voice seemed to
come from a long way off. I felt like I was
moving through a cold shallow pond. The
taller man took my elbow and led me to the
open doors of the van. I heard the other man
unzipping the silver bag. He prompted me.
"Do you know the deceased to be Mary Ann
Weathers?"

I looked up into his face, watching his
mouth move as he spoke. I thought of telling
him that until that very second I hadn't even
known her name.

The old woman's head was tipped back at
a sharp thirty-degree angle. It looked uncom-
fortable. There was no pillow under her neck.
Her eyelids were closed and her chin was
thrust up stiffly, like a store dummy's. She

was simply gone—I'd never seen anything go so far away. I felt my lips brush together to say something, but I doubted anyone could hear me. "I do," I whispered.

"Kindly sign here."

I signed where his forefinger pointed, square and pale skinned, with a clean, square fingernail. "I'm going home now," I said.

"You go on ahead," the man said, looking at my signature. "Sorry to trouble you. Thank you very much."

Both men were staring at me, so I tiptoed back to my car, moving softly and slowly so they wouldn't notice I wasn't wearing any shoes. I set my drink down in the street, and the paper cup tipped over; a stream of brown liquid ran down the gutter. I eased into my car, shut the door softly, and turned the key in the ignition. The engine roar flooded the air.

Across the way my own house was dark; a few lights floating here and there, one light burning at the side of the house. An unfamiliar car with rental plates was parked out front, surely my father's. I steered away from it as if it were a black hole to suck me in. In the rearview mirror I saw the two City of Richmond workers staring after my car.

I turned onto Monument and drove just a few yards before I pulled over. Then I lay down across the front seat, with my knees tucked up to my chest and my face just under the steering wheel. The sharp smell of gas filled the car. I wished I hadn't eaten those hamburgers. The damp air formed a pink halo around the street lamps, and the leaves hissed, fluttering whitish silver undersides. The car shook under my back. I sat up and shut off the engine.

My own watery reflection in the dark car window looked like a drowned girl's against the black glass. I stared deep into her eyes—one second they looked empty and blank, the next second shining and alive— till it no longer seemed as if the face had any relation to myself. I stared dispassionately through the glass. A long time passed. When I came back to myself I had a sensation of gravity rushing in, of space collapsing on it- self. I saw the old woman's body held between the men like a branch of silvery driftwood. Malachi reached out one long-fingered hand.

The driftwood spun beyond my reach, eddied in a slow circle, and moved downstream, bumping against rocks, gliding faster toward a roaring cataract, till I opened my eyes again and it was raining, the sound rushed against the roof of my father's car, and no one was there.

Chapter Eight

IT WAS STILL DARK, but loosening around the edges. The orange clock on the dashboard showed it was a little after four in the morning. I opened the glove compartment, and Malachi's black elastic bow tie dropped onto the floor, along with a few of my father's old pharmaceutical leaflets. I picked them up and looked at them. They were as glossy as advertisements for automobiles or exotic vacations, but inside were medical diagrams of diseased skeletons and muscle tissue, close-up photographs of lesions, deformed limbs.

I began searching through the car like an archaeologist digging in ancient catacombs. An outdated *Rand McNally Road Atlas* lay curled up fetus-style under the front seat, with my father's initials hand-lettered on the cover in his spiky black penmanship. At the back of the glove compartment was a half-empty box of Tic Tacs to sweeten his breath, the nub of a pencil, a torn parking stub from a Hilton in Raleigh, and a tiny spiral-bound notebook that had nothing written inside but dates and gas mileage in the ghost gray of pencil. I sat with this treasure perched on one shaking knee, watching the rain hammer the front windshield.

After a while I thumbed to the back of the notebook and wrote with the pencil nub, " 'My mother says indeed I am his. I for my part do not know. Nobody truly knows his own father.' <u>Homer.</u>" I closed the book and sat a while longer, holding it in my lap. I opened it again and added, "<u>Rilke:</u> 'How small is that with which we struggle: how great is that which struggles with us!' " The rain was beating steadily against the glass, almost in waves.

I opened the car door and splashed through puddles to the corner, where General Stuart stood gazing over the tops of the lamp-posts. My face was burning to the touch, and the black iron gate around the wet marble cooled my hand. Monument Avenue looked like the freshest place in Richmond, with all its cold white statues lined up like a row of refrigerators. General Jeb Stuart gave off a cool, bluish white light. When I leaned my head back to look up at him, he began sliding backward off his horse—tilting very gradually, almost in slow motion. I backed away. He stopped moving. I came close and reached out as if to touch the marble base. The fluorescent light from inside the statue filtered through my fingers so I could see the pulse jumping at my fingertips. It was strange I had never noticed those lights before. I brought the hand back to my face to ease what felt like the beginning of a fever.

"Go home," Jeb Stuart said. His whitish hair was pushed back in a lank, familiar way from his stony forehead. I could tell that his teeth were bad, under the closed mouth.

"Go home," the young general said again, in Walrus's voice, without moving his lips. He kept his eyes fixed on the purplish far horizon, where rain plunged like meteors into black puddles on the street.

The rain was windy; it fell in long, heavy

strokes, blowing the trees on Monument from right to left. I walked stooped over, as if I were carrying the rain on my back. Somewhere along the way a huge neighborhood dog fell in with me, shadowy under the downpour. It must have rained two inches in the time it took me to get down Monument, past my parked car, across to Vine, and over toward Gardenia. I put my head back and tried to watch the rain fall, but that made it feel as if I was going to fall backward, off my legs. The bottoms of my stockings were so badly torn it was like walking barefoot over gravel. The dog trotted alongside me, making a bass thrumming sound low in its throat.

The old woman's lights were off, but the porch lamp was on. Someone stood under it in a long white nightgown, waving at me over the railing. Rain poured in sheets off the porch roof in front of her. I ran up her front walk. "They told me you were dead!" I called.

The old woman tossed her arms up in the air and bent double, shaking with silent laughter. Suddenly one sleeve ripped loose and went rolling like tumbleweed across the wet porch. The scrap of silvery plastic stuck to the far wall and held there, whipping in the wind. I backed down her cracked front path and sprinted the last few yards home.

Then I was standing under the street lamp outside my house, the big dog panting beside me. The lamp's shivering, cast-down circle of light made an invisible umbrella for us to stand in. I turned up the collar of my jacket and let the rain beat steadily on the top of my head and across my shoulders.

One light was on upstairs in our house. I watched it, brushing rainwater out of my eyes, and after a long, dreamy time was rewarded by the sight of someone coming along the corridor, flitting from window to window like a worried moth. It was my mother, closing all the storm windows. I could see her from just the shoulders down, clad in a lilac-colored robe. The windows slid down one after another, with a familiar echoing bang and after rattle; a noise that had the quality of a dream because I'd heard it so many times in my childhood, lying in bed with all the other household sounds: her footsteps pausing outside my room in Connecticut to pull the chain of the attic fan, which would start up with its soft warbling, and then my father's footsteps, slower and heavier, stopping briefly outside my door and him calling, "Sweet dreams."

Now my mother leaned against a windowsill, looking out. Her long hair spilled over her shoulders like a girl's. I lifted one arm and waved. "Mom?"

I had been hanging on to the lamppost for support; when I let go, I nearly tumbled onto the asphalt, but she didn't see me. She was still kneeling at the window, gazing at some point above and behind my head. I turned to look and heard the window clatter shut upstairs. Then she was at the next window, closing that one, too, and then gone.

My hands were shaking around the lamppost. I put them out of sight into my jacket pockets and almost fell down again. I took the gold watch that Malachi had given me out of one pocket and held it to my ear to hear its rapid, steady *tick-tick-tick-tick*. The kitchen light burned bright yellow at the side of the house. Someone was waiting up. I reached out to touch the dog on its head, but it shied out of reach, then rubbed against my legs like a cat and disappeared completely, like a ghost. As I moved toward the house I couldn't feel the rain anymore. It was an insubstantial veil made of slanting silvery white lines of light. I moved carefully, skimming over the wet grass. Outside the porch I stopped and looked in.

My father was standing sideways to me at the kitchen sink. He looked older and taller, almost like a photograph of himself. We were standing perhaps three feet apart. He stood rubbing one hand along his heavily shadowed jaw. My hand crept up to touch my own face. He swung around toward me, holding a glass of water in one hand. I ducked out of sight. The kitchen chair scraped back, his water glass clicked down on the marble tabletop. All of my senses felt preternaturally alert. I could hear him breathing lightly through his nose as he drank, heard him swallow, then the wash of blood moving sluggishly past his tricky heart valve. I stood up and peered in through the doll-sized window, my face against the screen. The window was so small I had to look at him one little piece at a time. He sat with his chin sunk in one hand, his face turned toward the interior of the house.

The chain of the kitchen light hung straight down in front of him. He pulled on

it slowly, and even more slowly the room
bloomed into blackness around him. He set
the water glass down on the marble. I'd forgotten how melancholy-looking he was, and,
still, how charming. He could charm anybody—waiters, salespeople—and usually did.
Another lamp was on, farther back in the
house, and my mother came through the yellow rectangle of the doorway into the kitchen.
She said something that made my father smile
and turn around, and then they shifted on
their feet to face each other, and their arms
went up and around behind each other's
backs in slow motion, like dancers. Rain
dripped down the back of my neck. My parents walked out, holding hands, leaving the
room so empty it took my breath away.

Something close by was making a sharp
staccato sound; I listened for a minute—
my teeth were chattering. One looping bat,
signaler of dawn, flickered and swooped overhead, sailed under a phone wire, and disappeared.

Enough, I said to myself. I had to shake
free of whatever it was that stood between me
and my own happiness. It cost too much effort
to hold together this way, like a violin string

about to snap. I had to leave home; I had to leave Richmond, get on with my life. One way or another things were going to change, and keep on changing. The thought scared me so much that for a minute, standing there, I thought I was going to have a heart attack, that I had actually inherited my father's condition; I could feel a fiery slamming of my heart in the dead center of my chest.

Then I wasn't at the edge of the music anymore, looking down, but fell headfirst into its roaring. The bass chords struck and plummeted through the bottom of the universe and kept dropping, past sky, clouds, treetops—there was nothing to catch hold of. How can there be nothing? I thought. My own life. What is that? There were voices around me, inside the music, talking, coughing, making idle conversation. Somebody laughed. There were birds flying back up North, a green scarf, the smell of seawater. Nothing lost yet. A larger world, something besides the terror. I heard the rain stirring the leaves, striking the roof, hitting stones—something.

For one second the music fell in place, lit up in front of me like a movie, a night landscape flash-struck by lightning—still daylight

out there, green trees, blue sky—and the next
second all the long labor was still ahead; the
orchestration, the chorus, each of the instru-
mental parts, and having to copy it down note
after note.

I pushed open the screen door, took a few
steps with my hand out in the dark, and
bumped against marble. My father's water
glass sat in the middle of the kitchen table.
The silver crescent of water shimmered and
settled.

I reached for the water, but my hand
stopped in midair. I was afraid. I thought if I
drank it I'd die young, never marry at all, or
my children would be freaks. They'd have
weak hearts like my father, or they'd be ma-
lignant giants like me. A wall clock buzzed
angrily once, and then the shiny metal hands
on its face were visible and the red second
hand scurrying around.

I thought about my father's leather suitcases, already unpacked according to some
system, everything neatly put into drawers,
the luggage stowed toward the front of the
closet, ready for the next voyage out. Hanging
over my mother's rack of dress shoes, his
blue, or white, or blue-and-white-striped silky

cotton shirts would be gleaming from their wire hangers, solemn as judges, ready to slip away.

I pushed aside the glass of water. The hoop of white light swayed, brimmed, and burned, but didn't spill. My back muscles ached and when I coughed into my cupped hands, my breath scalded my palms. It felt like bronchitis.

Then for no reason I suddenly reached for the water, shut my eyes, and drank without stopping. I gripped the tumbler against irrational terror, taking smaller and smaller sips till there was nothing left but sweet air. I washed out the glass and set it ringing upside down on the drainer like a glass crown. Outside, the sky was a shimmering, flickering ultraviolet. As soon as the sun rose, I could go to sleep. Till then I felt I had to stand guard over the house and everyone sleeping in it. That was easy; the hard part would come later.

I took out some music paper. It was still very early.